*W*hat the critics are saying...

℘

5 hearts "Wow is all this reviewer can say after reading *Zylan Rebellion*. Ms. Wilde crafted a mesmerizing series that captures the imagination as well as the reader's hearts with her flair for dramatics as well as crafting a well-written storyline. Each of the books in the series can be read alone and by themselves but to get the whole picture of Zylar's Moons, read all three in order. Old characters and new ones abound here as the reader is swept away to Zylar and its many intriguing mysteries. From beginning to end, the reader is taken on a well-crafted ride that is sure to deliver a one-two punch at the end!" ~ *Dawn, Love Romances*

5 stars "I really enjoyed all the characters in this story. Tar, Nyssa, Mica and Tala, who are the main characters from the first two in this series, have a hand in helping Ahnika and Raj with their escapade. I also enjoyed the authors' attention to detail which brought a realistic feel to the story. Ms. Wilde also provides a Zylan Vocabulary at the end of the e-book, which I didn't need because of how thorough her explanations were. A definite keeper! I look forward to reading more from Ms. Wilde." ~ *Tallyn Porter, Just Erotic Romance*

RAVYN WILDE

ZYLAN
ZYLAR'S MOONS
REBELLION

ELLORA'S CAVE
ROMANTICA PUBLISHING

An Ellora's Cave Romantica Publication

www.ellorascave.com

Zylan Rebellion

Electronic book Publication 2005
Trade paperback Publication January 2006

Excerpt from *Let Them Eat Cake* Copyright © Ravyn Wilde, 2005

Warning:

The following material contains graphic sexual content meant for mature readers. *Zylan Rebellion* has been rated E–rotic by a minimum of three independent reviewers.

Ellora's Cave Publishing offers three levels of Romantica™ reading entertainment: S (S-ensuous), E (E-rotic), and X (X-treme).

S-*ensuous* love scenes are explicit and leave nothing to the imagination.

E-*rotic* love scenes are explicit, leave nothing to the imagination, and are high in volume per the overall word count. In addition, some E-rated titles might contain fantasy material that some readers find objectionable, such as bondage, submission, same sex encounters, forced seductions, and so forth. E-rated titles are the most graphic titles we carry; it is common, for instance, for an author to use words such as "fucking", "cock", "pussy", and such within their work of literature.

X-*treme* titles differ from E-rated titles only in plot premise and storyline execution. Unlike E-rated titles, stories designated with the letter X tend to contain controversial subject matter not for the faint of heart.

Also by Ravyn Wilde

ହେ

By the Book
Ellora's Cavemen: Tales from the Temple I *(Anthology)*
Ellora's Cavemen: Legendary Tails IV *(Anthology)*
Let Them Eat Cake
Men To Die For *(Anthololgy)*
Zylar's Moons 1: Zylan Captive
Zylar's Moons 2: Selven Refuge

Zylar's Moons:
Zylan Rebellion

ಎಂ

Dedication

~

This book is dedicated to my father. A love of books comes from many sources. Mine stems from growing up in a home where the bookshelves overflowed, and my father would lie on the floor of the living room—reading late into the night. I miss you, daddy.

Author Note

~

Readers, whether this is your first time on Zylar or a return visit...there is a vocabulary sheet on the following page to help with Zylan words and to keep you from feeling lost. If you haven't read the first two stories in this series, don't fret, the books can be read alone and still make sense. Welcome to the world of Zylar!

Ravyn

Trademarks Acknowledgement

~

The author acknowledges the trademarked status and trademark owners of the following wordmarks mentioned in this work of fiction:

Jacuzzi: Jacuzzi, Inc

Zylan Vocabulary

ॐ

Bi-non: day

Cid: flying craft

Duca: office

Glindash: auction

Jandai: village of women

Leonar: Lion

Lianon: city on Zmar where Nika lived.

Life Companion: husband or wife

Life cycles: years

Life mate: husband or wife

Link mate: husband or wife

Links: chains that are part of the body once a Zylan mates

Mecgots: little furry green animals on Zmar that are sometimes used for pets

Meoc: Zmar's ruling place

Minon: minute or moment

Moonflower: A highly scented flower that blooms at night

Nej: Spider-like insect that bites

Nilt: hour

Non: week

Nubes: Five males who serve the Selven. They have no apparent thought patterns or emotions.

Nui fruit: sweet and juicy pink fruit

Peela: Dragon-type bird

Ruling place: Tanar, where the palace is. Can also be used in place of palace.

Selven Refuge/gathering place: home of the Selven goddesses and priestesses

Selven goddess: highest level of training for the Selven

Selven priestess: goddess in training

Separate home: home away from the palace

Setnon: month

Shivet: Zylan swear word. Think screwed.

Soul trails: tendrils of color coming from a person's aura, can be used by Raj like fingerprints to identify and track someone

Tanar: ruling place, city of Nyssa and Tar

Vampen: strongly psychic person who "feeds" on another's life force through their orgasms

Vidar: large mountain crossroads village

Zelph: Raj and Mica's childhood home, Raj lives there now

Zmar: Ahnika's home planet, made up of mostly water

Prologue

❧

Sitting in the bow of the flat watercraft, Ahnika looked over the calm Zmarian Sea and marveled at the vibrant purple water lying quiet and still, glimmering like the finest crystal. The floating island looming in the distance appeared as a slight turquoise haze on the horizon. Zmar's single sun shone high in the green, cloudless sky and warmed her skin. A light breeze blew over the water, bringing with it the spicy-sweet smell of *Nui* fruit. It was the perfect time to be going out to gather herbs.

"Ahnika, make us some water sculptures," her youngest brother, Daza, demanded. At nine life cycles, he didn't possess the temperament for just enjoying the view. She glanced at Niko. Neither did a boy of twelve. Smiling at them, she nodded.

Unconsciously, she entertained her two younger brothers by using her talents to make figures from the water. Zmar was a planet comprised of over eighty percent of the liquid—so most of her people learned the art of creating water shapes with their minds by puberty. The activity was so simple—it required no concentration.

She formed the water into sea creatures, real and imagined, made faces appear and manufactured land animals...and let her mind drift. It should have been the perfect *bi-non* to enjoy being out in the sun where she could revel in the rare opportunity to visit one of the unclaimed pieces of land. She would be able to run wild on the grass and in the forest and get away from people stacked on top of each other.

Instead she felt…distracted. Some dark presence seemed to almost permeate the air surrounding her and she couldn't shake the feeling that something was wrong. Unable to pinpoint the reason for her uneasiness, she worried even more.

Her instincts screamed to abandon the trip and return home. Immediately. Skin prickling with growing alarm, she felt as if she were being warned of danger lying just ahead. But what danger? Her frustration level grew as her eyes darted over the vast, *empty* sea. It was useless to speculate. Whatever forewarning was being sent her way was wasted. Since she was just reaching maturity, she was too young to have developed any precognitive abilities. Such powers could come to her, but it would take a long while to learn what they meant. In the meantime, she had no way of knowing why she felt this way.

Sighing, she mentally pushed her agitation away and chose to believe she was just being fanciful. Or restless and torn because she would soon start making the rounds of claiming parties. The first of the celebrations she'd be attending would be on Zmar and if she didn't discover her mate on her own world, then eventually she'd be taken to Zylar, their mother planet.

Her divided emotions must be the cause of her restlessness. In the time it took for two heartbeats she fluctuated between excitement and dread, very hesitant to move on with her life. Not that she didn't want a mate, she just yearned for something more. She really didn't want to go from her parents' overprotective home to a Life Companion's. Yet, when she closed her eyes, she could almost sense him somewhere out there waiting for her.

Imagining a man with flowing dark hair and enticingly golden skin, whose shockingly pale blue gaze would steal her breath, she questioned her sanity when she could see him so clearly in her mind's eye.

She'd even allowed herself to wonder what their children would look like.

Would they have the pale pink tones of her flesh or would they be a beautiful tan like their father? Stupid thought. She reminded herself that she didn't even want a mate, nor did she have the slightest idea of what he would look like when she got one.

"Who's that, Nika?" Daza asked.

Looking at her brother in question, she realized he was focused on the water. Glancing over to see what caught his attention, her eyes opened wide and she gasped in shock. While she'd been dreaming, she'd unconsciously formed an aquatic sculpture in the shape of a man's head. Not anyone Daza would recognize...but she sure did.

If she replaced the purple water with dark hair and lightly bronzed skin, it would be the man she'd just been dreaming about. The man she'd foolishly decided must be her mate. She was losing her mind. First she thought she'd gained some sort of precognitive ability, imagining some horrible danger, and now she was inventing people.

"Ahnika, are you all right?" Jannela's soft voice intruded on her thoughts.

Her friend looked worried. She gave Janey a weak smile and said, "I am fine. I just feel a little—I don't know—nervous for some reason. Like something bad is about to happen to us. Do you feel anything?"

Janey shook her head. "No, but that shouldn't surprise you as neither one of us has any powers to speak of. Do you think we should tell the herb woman we need to turn back and forget about gathering medicinal plants this *bi-non*?"

"On what basis? That I feel as if a million bugs are crawling over my skin? You know how much attention she would pay to warnings from someone not known to have any precog skills. This is the first time for many *nons* the weather has been nice enough to allow us to go to the far island for harvesting. No, just keep your eyes on the boys for me while we are on land, would you? Niko and Daza are going to want to see if all their treasures are intact so I'd appreciate it if you would take them to their little hidey-hole for a bit. I'll help the women and try to push them to finish as fast as possible. Just don't stay away too long. I've got a bad feeling and I want to get back home as soon as we can."

"Sure, I'll be glad to take them. That'll be fun. Okay then, let's change the subject and see if we can't get you in a better mood. Did your father tell you if you are going with him to Zylar at the end of this moon cycle?" Janey asked in blatant eagerness.

"He isn't sure yet. Something's bothering him and he said it would be best if I go to my first claiming parties on Zmar. He feels there's no reason for me to go planet-hopping if my mate is here." She sighed. "I'm sure he's right...but, somehow...I just don't think I'm going to find a Life Companion on Zmar and I want to spend time under Zylar's moons." And not being allowed to go irritated her because she knew the ancients taught that true psychic potential never emerged until you spent time under those three moons. Zmarians had migrated from Zylar and kept most of their physical characteristics except for the added pigmentation in our skin. Most psychic abilities just didn't seem to show up until you'd been on Zylar.

Janey just shrugged.

Ahnika continued thoughtfully, "Unfortunately, my father doesn't think it's necessary for me to worry about any possible psi-abilities I might discover. It is so unfair—they've already made plans to take each of the boys to Zylar for a month when they reach puberty to give them a dose of the moons. They've never even considered such a trip for me," she lamented.

"I know. My parents did the same. *All* the boys from Zmar are taken to Zylar to spend a *setnon's* cycle under the moons, but it is not believed to be a needed expense for the daughters. You know our parents figure we'll get all the power we'll need once we're mated."

Ahnika snorted, "Well, I don't think I like the obvious inequality. Even my mother just tells me it will all work out and not to worry. She promises me I'll find my power and then she smiles knowingly. I *hate* that! How can I uncover my abilities if I don't go to Zylar?"

Janey giggled. "Maybe she is talking about an entirely different kind of power. The kind that starts and ends with making your mate happy, with keeping his life—"

Ahnika chimed in, "—serene and calm, a home filled with warmth and children. A place to escape from his duties…" They both burst out laughing. As young girls they had often been chastised for failing to use the proper tone of respect when repeating this portion of the Mating Creed during their studies. Their parents took the ancient writings *very* seriously.

Neither of them understood why the sentiment was so irritating. A female's life followed a very preordained path. Ahnika didn't have any options. She was expected to place herself in front of eligible males, find her mate, bear his children, and then keep their home a refuge from the outside world. It was all she'd been trained to do. All she and Janey were expected to do. Why should the thought grate on her every nerve? She didn't have a choice, as this wasn't about her or what *she* wanted, it was all she could ask from her life. Her thoughts were tumultuous, forever shifting between wanting something more and the anticipation of finding the one man who could claim her. She wanted her own home and children. Since her birth, this time of her life had been talked about and planned. She'd been grilled with painstaking thoroughness on mate protocol and highborn social customs...and, recently, been measured and fitted for new gowns to wear to the social gatherings.

Lately the whispers of unexplained promise seemed to constantly tease the fringes of her mind. Those faint rustlings worked on her psyche, pushing her in a direction she wasn't certain she wanted to go. And the sneaky beguilement irritated her as she had no idea where to start looking for the one man who would call the links from her body. Until her new feelings made more sense, she would do the accepted thing—go to the claiming parties and look pretty in case some man came up to her and said, "You're mine."

Dreaming of a golden-skinned man with long dark hair and icy blue eyes, whom she hoped might allow her a little more freedom than she received from her parents, only confused her. Were the dreams just foolish imaginings...or something else?

On Zmar, she wouldn't be allowed the chance to question her fate. There would be no adventure or time to figure out what she wanted in life. Since she didn't have any idea what she did want, how could she argue with tradition? No. It was her duty to make herself available to the men of Zmar and, if no mate were found on this planet, then she would be taken to Zylar to be put on display there. And if a little voice inside her head asked *why*? Well, she'd subdued the nagging influence before.

Pulling herself away from her depressing thoughts, she watched in mounting trepidation as the gathering area appeared. For several *minons* she'd been focused on her inner conflict, but now her agitation returned.

Maybe her uneasiness just stemmed from the thought of being on land with only a small number of people in the gathering party. Being with so few people never bothered her before. Normally she loved getting away from the cramped environs of her home and going into the wild. She lived in Lianon, the ruling city in this district, and the entire area was designed so every square inch of dirt contained a multistoried building to house the population. The land was much too valuable to be used for growing food or for having space for roaming.

Container gardens were located on the rooftops of each building for growing their food. Here and there, small patches of blue grass were left bare so small children had a space to play. Sometimes, she thought sadly, it would be wonderful to live in a place where she could run barefoot in the grass, stop and smell flowers or just take a few *minons* to enjoy being outside without being caught up in the crush of people that seemed to be everywhere at once.

No. It wasn't the lack of bodies that bothered her.

Her father managed this area as Chancellor. In charge of keeping the peace and settling disputes in their region, he reported directly to the Ruler of Zmar. The ruling place for Zmar was half a planet away in a city called Meoc. She assumed Meoc would be the first place her father would take her for a claiming party. Zmar, in turn, owed allegiance to the Ruler of Zylar—and she was back to thinking of finding a mate. *Shivet*...she needed to concentrate on where they were going.

Father wouldn't have let them come out this *bi-non* if there were any problems to be concerned about. Blessed with strong precognitive abilities, surely he would have known if the gathering party would be in any danger. Although she couldn't help reminding herself of the times he'd explained to her that he couldn't see *everything* and how sometimes events were meant to happen without interference.

Their destination was an island left solely to the wild. This uninhabited space allowed the plants and few land animals on Zmar free rein. As they approached, she scanned the area with worried care. Her anxiety increased as they landed the boat on the soft black sand beach. Besides Ahnika, her brothers and Janey, the little gathering party was made up of three elders—women known for their healing abilities, and two other girls who were a few life cycles older than Ahnika. Lianon had so many people living in it that she had no way of knowing everyone who lived within its cramped protection. From the young women's conversation, she did know they had already started the social flurry of looking for a mate.

Harvesting groups never took guards with them. Ahnika decided she would talk to her father about her uneasiness during this trip and suggest he assign at least one or two guards to each party. In her entire life there'd never been even the hint of a problem, but it didn't matter—the isolated island could hide an army.

She didn't see or hear anything out of the ordinary. The beach they landed on appeared clear of footprints and the small clearing they were in this *bi-non* was filled with nothing but swaying blue sage grass. The multicolored wild herbs were in bloom and she could see the peaceful *mecgots*, the little green furry creatures Zmarians often tamed for pets, tumbling in the distance. The scene couldn't have been any more peaceful.

Sighing, she started toward the colorful riot of flowering herbs, nothing seemed out of place in the little glade so she assumed her imagination was playing tricks on her and relaxed. Laughing at her brothers' urgency to go exploring, she waved goodbye to Janey and the boys after making them promise to stay together. She kept her eyes on them until they disappeared into the turquoise forest and then she turned her energies to making the accumulation of herbs go as quickly as possible. She wandered close to the thick woods and stopped every few *minons* to watch and listen. It was obvious there wasn't anything for her to worry about.

* * * * *

Minons later she was roughly grabbed from behind. Glancing down, she saw deep red cloth covering powerful arms that were holding her immobile. As she fought her assailant, she heard screams and sounds from the other women as they struggled against a threat Ahnika couldn't see and their terrified cries echoed throughout the clearing. A deep male voice shouted something about making sure the women they took were free of links.

"They need to be young enough to train..."

Wildly kicking and thrashing her body in an effort to dislodge the man confining her, she managed to whack him with her head and he dropped her to the ground. Turning over onto her back, she stumbled to her feet and, looking around her, she couldn't believe what her eyes were seeing. These men wore tunics embroidered with the Zylan Ruler's crest! Before she could gather her wits and run, the man who had grabbed her raised his fist and struck the side of her head near her temple.

Fighting to remain conscious after the vicious blow to her head, disbelief roared in her mind. The hysterical notion that she should have been more careful what she wished for surfaced. As her eyes closed in pain, she felt tears falling. It didn't look like she would ever get the opportunity to find the man in the water silhouette.

Chapter One
Two life cycles later

&

She was so cold. As she lay in the dark, her body separated from the stone floor by a deplorably thin pallet, Ahnika considered her options. Death would be preferable to the current nightmare of pain, fear and degradation she'd lived through in the last two life cycles. She was so tired of fighting her tormentors. She could think of nothing beyond being released from her suffering and she found herself praying almost fanatically for freedom—even if liberation came with death. Without some form of escape, she knew what would come—her future would be filled with continuous torture.

The scream startled her to her feet. *Oh, Goddess! It was starting again.* She seldom saw the other women who shared her prison. Everyone was kept locked in separate cells, alone and neglected. Unless it was her turn for "training" or her captors compelled her to observe another's torture, she was left alone with the chilling screams, and her imagination. Considering all the things she'd seen done in this prison, her imagination was a horrible companion. The beatings and bodily torture paled in comparison to the unnatural torment the women were forced to go through.

Sobs racked her slender, badly bruised body, causing her to double over with grief. She fell to her knees and buried her face in her hands, taking no comfort in the blanket of hair shielding her as it provided no protection. "Please, Goddess. Help me, please help us all," she cried in heartfelt supplication. "I can't take any more."

She couldn't keep her thoughts from turning inward and back two life cycles, as she tried desperately to recapture the carefree times on her home planet Zmar. She'd been nineteen life cycles old, happy and well-loved by her family. Wanting to go back and relive that time, she wished she'd listened to her inner warnings and focused on what her parents had planned for her.

Instead of being happy with her lot in life, she'd wanted an adventure and time to discover her talents and strengths. She thought her father insensitive to her needs. Her mind had been divided between yearnings for individual freedom, and a compulsion to let tradition guide her. She'd been looking forward to coming of age and spending time visiting other planets and worlds. Knew she was supposed to find her link-mate, but she also wanted time to concentrate on developing her individual gifts and abilities before she tied herself to a mate who would continue molding her into the perfect Zmarian woman.

Now her musings seemed foolish. What she wouldn't give to just go back and start over. To listen to her parents and revel in the safe and secure if somewhat restricted lifestyle. Tears flowed from her eyes as she grimaced with regret. She hadn't understood how much freedom she'd really enjoyed.

Looking back, she remembered hearing rumors, little whispered comments about women disappearing and the Zylan leader's involvement in some sort of slaving trade. She never imagined the stories to be true or that she could be caught in the nightmare.

She hadn't been the only one to ignore the gossip surrounding the Zylan Ruler's reprehensible actions. If anyone had believed the stories, she and the other women of Zmar wouldn't have been allowed to participate in a gathering trip without protection.

But the men invading her planet that long ago *bi-non* wore the royal crest on their tunics. Once she'd regained consciousness, the men took great pains to tell her how no one could stop them, as guards of the powerful Zylan Ruler they were untouchable. Ahnika had been captured along with two other young women from her village and then taken aboard a ship. The three girls were kept apart, so she had no idea what happened to them once they reached their destination. She'd never seen them again.

Nor could she find out what had been done to the others in the gathering trip. Had they been left alone? Killed? Not knowing the fate of her brothers and Janey almost drove her mad—she'd prayed long and hard that her brothers and friend had escaped the insanity of that day. She may never learn if they were alive or dead.

She knew she'd been taken to Zylar only because she caught a quick glimpse of Zylar's three moons when she was being moved into this prison.

At first, her life here was mind-numbingly solitary. For the initial life cycle, she'd been locked away in a small, deep, underground cell. There was little light, no fresh air and no one to talk to. Miserable and lonely, the only people she saw were the few watchers who were assigned to walk her back and forth to a bathing pool. She hadn't been allowed to communicate with them, and swimming in the deep underground pool had been her only escape from the tiny rock chamber and her sole form of exercise. With one dress to wear, she would wash it in the pool before cleansing her body and when her time in the water came to an end, she would put on the wet rag and return to her cell where she would spend several *bi-nons* uncomfortable and cold in the dripping garment.

The nights were filled with muffled weeping coming from the other cells lining the hall. When the screaming started, she hadn't understood what was happening around her and many times she'd cried herself to sleep in self-pity and fear. She wanted someone to come and rescue her from this madness.

She hadn't known how bad it was going to get.

She flinched when she remembered the first time her door had opened during what she assumed was night. Even though she had no way to see the suns rising and falling from her cell, there was an ebb and flow to this place she used to distinguish the passing of time. Groggy and disorientated, Ahnika had been completely thrown by the unusual event of having a visitor shortly after her meal of stringy meat and stale bread. The change in routine gave her a burst of hope, believing that — somehow — someone had found her.

Her hope had quickly turned to disbelief and then to abject terror. The man at the door had jerked her off the pallet and dragged her unceremoniously to a room at the end of the hall. This room was larger and brighter than her cell, the light from several bright orbs added to her disorientation. With tears streaming from her eyes, it took her many *minons* before she could see and understand the horror awaiting her.

Waiting for her in the rock chamber were two people — a woman dressed much like herself in a tattered gown falling loose around a frail body, her demeanor of downcast eyes and drooping shoulders radiated despair and pain. She didn't acknowledge Ahnika's presence in any way.

The guard who'd brought her to the small chamber was dressed in a simple dark tunic and pants. He stepped back and looked toward the second man in the room — the person obviously in charge. Ahnika turned her attention to this man. Clearly a man of wealth and position, he was the most imposing person she'd ever seen. Tall, regally dressed, with odd-colored hair — black with strange copper highlights — he caught and held her gaze. She studied him for several *minons*, wondering if his hair color signified some sort of special powers. The true nightmare began when he opened his mouth.

"What is your name, girl?" he demanded coldly.

Bewildered, she shifted her vision, looking at him in silent dismay. It had been so very long since anyone had spoken to her. In all her time in captivity, no one had ever asked her a question. They ordered her to the bathing pool or told her to be quiet…talking was not allowed. *Her name*?

He slapped her. Hard. "Answer me when I speak to you!"

Ahnika's head snapped back and her eyes welled with tears. She could feel the pain and the heat from his hand on her cheek. That slap destroyed the optimism she'd been desperately clinging to, that somehow, after all this time, she'd been rescued. "Ahnika," she replied in broken despair.

The man glowered at her. His eyes were deep, black wells of hatred. "Ahnika," he spat out. "Listen closely and heed me well, Ahnika. You will start your training tonight. In the beginning, you will be present to observe and to learn what is expected of you. Later, you will participate in activities intended to educate you on your new life. Any and all disobedience will be punished with pain."

"I don't understand. What training?" she started to ask.

Crack.

He backhanded her, this time splitting her lip. The taste of blood in her mouth was a nauseating illustration of what she had to look forward to.

"First lesson. You do not speak unless you are asked a direct question," he growled menacingly. "You will listen and watch and do only what you are told. Do you understand me?"

Oh, yeah. She understood she was in big trouble. This man frightened her with his intensity and his obvious enjoyment of her suffering. The pain in her head and the taste of blood in her mouth made her position very clear. She wasn't stupid. She kept her eyes lowered and said what he wanted to hear. "Yes."

His next question confused her. "Do you know what mating links are?"

Was this a trick question? Why wouldn't she know what mating links were? Unless he didn't know she came from Zmar. A Zmarian's physical makeup was the same as those on Zylar, except for their different skin coloring. He couldn't miss the red pigmentation marking her as a native of Zmar, could he? Then she remembered her father telling her once how Zylar had an assortment of people, explaining she'd see all types of skin coloration and body types. Not everyone with red skin would be Zmarian. *Goddess she missed her father and his stories.*

And why was this man asking her about the links? Mate links were small, delicate gold chains created within a Zylan or Zmarian body when they mated with their true Life Companion. The links were part of everyone's internal makeup, but they only made an external physical appearance when you found your one true mate. Once this happened, the link-chains would come into being at the male and female's breasts, around their waists and through their sexual organs. The chains ensured a couple's happiness by giving them a perceptive window into each other's needs. The links heightened sexual pleasure and served as a visible sign of being mated.

Well, she certainly wasn't going to ask why he questioned her on them. "Yes, I know what they are," she replied with careful restraint, trying to keep her tone of voice flat.

"Good, then we can skip that part. The *blessed* things are useless. In the past, a woman was at least somewhat under her mate's control. Not to the degree they should have been, but I've found a way around the leniency the links allowed. I've discovered a way to give men a choice of mate, rather than letting nature decide who their mates would be. All that crap about not being able to do anything but see to their mate's happiness because of the links' connection is ridiculous. A man's happiness is what is important. Not a woman's. But now...now my services are even more significant, since women think they should be allowed to control..."

At this point he started ranting about women who didn't know their place, women who thought they had a right to use their own power and made no attempt to surrender to their husband's command.

His vision of how the planet should be governed frightened her. *Who was this man?*

Ahnika kept quiet, her mind unable to cope with the strain of his fanaticism and the alteration of her solitary routine. She had no idea what he was raging about. Wondering if he'd forgotten about her and the other woman, she couldn't tell if his comments were directed toward any one person in the room. He wasn't making sense and the more he talked, the crazier he seemed to become. Spittle formed at the corners of his mouth and his eyes seemed to glaze over.

His view of a woman's place seemed to be one of pain and silent suffering. Her face hurt where he'd hit her, and her exhausted body trembled from this little mental game. Glancing surreptitiously around the cold room, she tried to see if anything would give her an idea of where she was or what he could be rambling about. But, like her private cell, there were no windows and the larger chamber held no answers for her.

The room contained a single platform with a pallet, and several sets of shackles on the wall. A low shelf was lined with scary, sharp-looking implements. A shudder ran through her body, seeing the evil-looking instruments made her more afraid than ever.

"But I fixed it," the man gloated.

Oh, great. While she'd been looking around the room, she'd lost track of what he'd been saying.

"...And, to prove my point, I'll give you a little demonstration. Zabeth...disrobe." Without raising her eyes or making any comment, the other woman stripped down to bare skin. In shock at this occurrence, Ahnika couldn't help but see that Zabeth was a linked woman. Her link chains hung from red and angrily swollen nipples.

Ahnika frowned. Link chains weren't supposed to get infected or cause irritation. *Could Zabeth be the Life Companion to this beast of a man?* Ahnika suddenly felt sorry for her.

"She looks like a true-linked woman, doesn't she?" came the sly question.

"Yes." Ahnika was so confused about what had happened and why she was here, that she decided to stick to yes and no answers. Period.

"Well, she is linked the way she should be bound — totally at her mate's mercy. She is linked without having to form a true physical bond." He grinned evilly. "I created those links. I forced her body to accept them and now, if I get tired of her, any man who pays the price can take her for his mate, without the risk of getting a female he can't fully control," he said proudly.

Once more she didn't comprehend what he was talking about. Unfortunately, a few *minons* later he showed her.

Pulling a small black box from a pocket in his tunic, he pressed a button. Immediately Zabeth screamed in pain. She clutched at her chest and fell to the ground writhing in agony. He had used the small device to create what appeared to be a tremendous amount of pain in her links.

Ahnika's hand flew up to cover her mouth, as she suddenly understood the nightmarish screams she'd heard over the past *setnons* and why the kidnappers only bothered taking women who had not yet been linked — "Young enough to train," she'd heard one slaver say. "Young enough to train…"

Unable to fathom the anguish and pain the women in the adjoining cells had been forced to endure, she fought to keep from screaming herself. She was going to be sick. When he barked an order for the poor woman to get up on her knees and take the guard's cock into her mouth and demonstrate her skill, Zabeth followed the orders without hesitation.

Ahnika had been forced to watch. When she tried to turn away and hide her eyes, the horrid man slapped her again. Only when she started retching did he dismiss her and demand the guard take her back to her cell. Snarling and angry at having been forced to leave the torture chamber, the guard vented his frustration and rage on Ahnika by using every *minon* of the journey back to her private prison to slap, pinch or kick her.

Crawling to her pallet after she'd thrown up in a corner, she succumbed to the sobs racking her body. She'd cried tears for poor Zabeth, and for what she knew would eventually happen to her if she couldn't find some way to leave this dreadful place.

Over the following *setnons*, variations of this night played out in unbelievable ways. The circumstances and rules of her current nightmare had been made very clear. Their captor was a monster who had somehow found a way to create false link chains he could — and did — implant within a woman's body. While the metal links he'd fashioned looked very real, they were unnatural imitations meant to mimic the legitimate physical links, which formed when Life Companions mated.

He specifically made the chains to cause pain and to ensure a woman's complete and total submission. During her captivity, she'd been forced to watch the procedure where his false links were attached to other girls. She had been heartsick to see the loss of blood and the torment the women went through as the chains were threaded first through their nipples, then around the waist and, horribly, through their genitalia. Once the links were in place, she watched as women who'd resisted and been beaten for their failure to comply, now scrambled to fulfill the kidnappers' commands. She feared she'd be broken like the others before her.

After observing the torturous procedure, she'd come to a decision. If the women were forced to accept the pain and humiliation...she could somehow find the strength to witness their torment with dignity and proud forbearance. Unable to belittle their trials with her own weakness and fear, she watched and remembered *for* them, and, Goddess willing, some *bi-non* soon, she would try to find a way to help them all.

When they tried to force her to pleasure a man, she refused. When she wouldn't touch or respond to their ministrations, she was whipped. From a guard's comment during one of her trainings, she'd learned that her value would be diminished if her virginity were taken, so she didn't have to worry about being raped in addition to everything else she was put through. With this knowledge came some strength. Praying each time she was beaten that her body would heal, she continued to resist their demands. She realized once the false links were put in place, she would be unable to do so.

She hadn't understood how the decision was made as to who would be trained next or when the links were to be implanted. There didn't seem to be a master plan until she discovered the nightmare only started with the mutilation of the women's bodies.

As if the pain and physical torture weren't enough, once the girls were trained in sexual submissiveness, they were then sold to the highest bidder. Ahnika had been *required* to watch the last auction. She'd seen the assembled men inspect each girl and comment on how their hair and physical characteristics met specific requirements.

Links were embedded within the women once the demon had at least one potential buyer and then those girls were featured at the next auction. Evidently he didn't put the chains in earlier because there had been times in the past when the false links and the pain they caused completely broke a woman's spirit. It seemed his customers wanted the appearance of being the one to finish their purchased mate's training. The men wanted a little fight in their women…at least a fight they could control.

She was next. A buyer had been located who liked red skin and, if she didn't get away now, her false links would be put in place at suns rise. There would be no other chance for escape and she would be in the next auction.

The thought of enduring the public spectacle, of standing naked and exposed on the auction block, her body accessible to the fondling and probing of interested buyers, made her believe death would be a viable option. From what she'd seen during the appalling demonstration, the men weren't allowed to take the girl's virginity but they could do just about anything else while they inspected the merchandise being offered.

Once a bid was accepted, the girl's new master would control the level of pain sent to the false links through a black box he kept hidden in his pocket. This device allowed the new owner to manipulate his newly purchased *mate* and compel total obedience, including submission to whatever sexual act he desired. The exhibition of control and depravity following the men's selections had traumatized her very soul. Successful buyers were encouraged to use the box and demonstrate how well it worked on their choice of mate.

The final act for the newly *mated* men at the auction was to have their nipples pierced and a parody of mating links threaded through the new holes. These piercings were for looks only. To make it appear each man was truly mated. There were no ties to any box to create pain, nor did they have their genitals pierced. The process was done solely to allow the men to wear the traditional mating garments showing the chains hanging from their nipples. Everyone would believe they were truly mated.

It was demoralizing to realize these auctions had been going on for many life cycles. This man had ruined the lives of many women.

Ahnika came back to herself lying curled in a tight ball on the floor of her cell. She had one chance for freedom and it would be very risky. If she were caught, it could mean her death. Knowing this, she still decided to try and escape. She *wanted* them to kill her if she failed. Couldn't bear the thought of being false-linked to a man whose thrills in life would come from causing her pain and forcing her into total submission.

She'd devised the plan *setnons* ago, but the beatings she received kept her too weak to make an attempt. Now that they wanted her strong enough to live through having links added to her body, they'd left her alone to heal and gather strength. She was still sore and bruised, but well enough for what she needed to do.

Her cell door opened.

Heart lurching in her chest she was unable to control the fear snaking through her limbs. She stood up on trembling legs and slowly walked from the small underground chamber, down the long, dark tunnel to the bathing pools. She tried to swallow around the constriction in her throat and calm her pulse as it throbbed in frantic anticipation. This was it…she'd run out of time.

Before tonight, she'd only been in the pools when the light from Zylar's two suns shown through an opening at the top. It had been the only natural light she'd seen since being kidnapped. Because they wanted her clean for the early morning procedure to add the links, she was being taken to the pool at night. The torchlight flickering on the walls cast moving shadows on the water and she prayed the shifting light would make it harder to see and help conceal her from the eyes of her watcher.

Fear had been a part of her life for the past two life cycles and she knew it intimately. Everything centered on her ability to work through her panic. Shaking inside, so afraid of failing this all-important attempt, she tried to concentrate on her surroundings.

Surveying the pool that had been her only refuge, she stole a surreptitious glance at old Alma, her watcher for tonight. Good. As she'd hoped, Alma was sitting on a large rock and leaning against the wall at the entrance, already dozing. Perfect. Alma was the one usually assigned as her watcher and there had been many times the two of them had repeated this scenario. Alma depended on Ahnika to wake her from her nap when it was time to go. *Well, not this time* With luck, Alma would sleep until the suns rise.

Knowing that Alma would be severely punished if the escape were successful, Ahnika buried her guilt. The old woman knew the prisoners kept in the cells weren't there because they wanted to be…and she was well aware of the pain and suffering all the women were required to go through. Ahnika refused to feel remorse in running for her life.

Over the last several *setnons*, Ahnika had stayed beneath the water longer and swam farther from the entrance to the cells. Initially, there'd been small panic attacks among her watchers when she remained submerged for increased periods of time. But she calmly explained that, on her planet, it was normal to stay underwater for so long.

Zmarians were born with special abilities to hold their breath. Never staying under as long as she was able, each attempt lasted just a few *minons*...any longer and she would be taking a risk that someone would figure out how she ultimately disappeared. *If it worked.* Eventually the watchers became used to her ways and let her have this one freedom, to do this one *small thing* They had no understanding of her world or her people's physical makeup and this lack of knowledge would work in her favor.

Ahnika snorted under her breath as she stepped, naked, into the embrace of cool, clean water. More water than land, her home world's environment had changed Zmarian physiology to adapt to their liquid surroundings. The red pigmentation of her skin allowed her to absorb oxygen within each pore and store it for later use. Zmarians were also born with increased lung capacity, and had the ability to hold their breath for extremely long periods of time. *Small thing*? Both of these traits meant she could stay underwater for over a *nilt*.

Ahnika swam out a little from the bank and dove deep, staying submerged for several *minons*. She quietly broke the surface of the dark lavender water and quickly glanced at the old watcher. The resting woman hadn't moved.

Silently she made her way to the other side of the underground pool. Several *setnons* ago, while swimming close to the walls, she'd discovered an opening in the rock below the water's surface. The hole appeared to be a below ground river feeding the small subterranean lake in this chamber. She hoped it was a tunnel with an exit and not—please, Goddess—just a short passage that would dump her into an inner courtyard within this prison. She'd followed the water's path in her mind, but tracing its entire length reached beyond her psychic abilities. She could only guess not being able to "see" where it ended was a good thing—she needed a way through to the outside world.

Before diving deep, she took a deep breath and then slid determinedly into the tunnel, her mind turned firmly away from terror and possible death.

There was no light or way for her to see what awaited her. Moving slowly with her arms stretched in front of her, she closed her eyes tight. With her eyes open she kept struggling to *see* and the mental war robbed her of needed strength. Several times she started to panic, her mind screaming in denial as her air reserves ran low and her body protested its lack of oxygen. Each time, just as she'd decided she would die in this water-clogged cemetery, she would miraculously find a small pocket of air, which allowed her a few *minons* to rest and breathe.

Stale and barely breathable, those small gulps of air still meant the difference between life and death and ensured her freedom. Each victory provided enough encouragement to fuel her resolve to keep going and Ahnika followed the underground tunnel, losing any sense of time.

At long last, the water dumped her into a cold, outside lake. The fresh air and the reality of being outside for the first time in two life cycles devastated her emotions. Crawling to shore, she lay for a very long time sobbing quietly in the soft blue grass. When she finally managed to get herself under control, she rolled onto her back and looked in awe at the night sky. She'd escaped her tormentors and, at least for now, she was free!

Hugging her arms around her bare chest, she grinned like a lunatic. Her luck seemed to have changed and she would be able to keep running.

Above her, shining full and bright as omens of hope, Zylar's three gorgeous moons were ready to light her way.

Chapter Two

ဆာ

Raj went to meet with his client, Brac. The man lived in a large stone stronghold that differed greatly from the usual Zylan dwellings. Colorful and warm, homes in Tanar were normally fashioned of wood. Each family used shades of a specific color to set them apart...a son's house was painted a lighter shade of blue than the father's, for instance.

But this rock structure was ugly and depressing, its size and the lack of windows or any coloration marked it as a sinister fortress. The only other structure made of stone in Tanar was the ruling place, however, the two buildings appeared to be polar opposites. The palace had windows and colorful banners on the outer walls, with flowering plants and small blue grass areas for sitting outside. Brac's home had no color, no windows and the surrounding area was nothing more than dirt and rocks.

Reaching out with his psychic conscience, he was surprised to find that the rock walls of the fortress seemed to somehow suppress emotions, as if they were shielding secrets. He could sense despair radiating from within, along with sensations of pain, sadness and fear. But the feelings were vague, as if they weren't coming from a specific person...but resonated from within.

As a servant let Raj into the building, he cursed his weakened state. Regretted his decision to delay recharging his psychic power after his last job because he hadn't thought he'd need to feed before meeting with Brac. The request to locate a missing daughter seemed a very simple quest and hadn't triggered any alarms. Well, now the alarms were ringing loud and clear and he really wished he were at full strength.

Brac was a member of the Ruling Council of Ten on Zylar. The Ten were chosen for their individual psychic strength and strong moral character to assist Tar, Zylar's Ruler, in governing the planet. Mica, Raj's brother was in charge of the Ruling Council. Raj didn't usually worry about planet politics—that was his brother's problem. But he'd heard enough to know Mica wasn't happy with Brac. They had a history of constant disagreement over moral and political issues. Brac always seemed to be in competition with Mica, at least in Brac's own mind.

Most of Brac's competitive attitude stemmed from his jealousy over Mica's position as High Priest of Zylar. On Zylar, a person's hair color often signified special powers or gifts. Both Mica and Brac were born with black hair streaked with vivid copper highlights. This color signified one of the mystical characteristics indicating those born gifted and possibly destined to become High Priest. Brac's streaks were a little more subdued and—unfortunately for Brac—he lacked the most important indicator that a person possessed the entire set of characteristics required for the honor of High Priest. He hadn't been able to speak at birth.

Raj remembered hearing how much Brac had hated not being born with this inherent knowledge as Mica had been. Somehow Raj didn't think Brac would hire him if he realized Mica was his brother and he wasn't going to volunteer the information.

When Brac finally called him into his *duca*, the psychic sensations Raj got from both the man and his home bothered him deeply. Looking around the small room, he nodded to the man sitting behind the desk. He would need to be alert. Careful. Something wasn't right in this place. He couldn't put a specific name or location to the impressions he felt. But one emotion — misery — almost overwhelmed him with its intensity.

While the other psychic imprints battering at his tired mind were suppressed and obscure, the man in front of him clearly emitted waves of self-importance and arrogance — he was full of himself. Raj knew there was more to Brac than met the eye — more to this place. He didn't intend to jeopardize the assignment from Brac to hunt for his daughter. Something was wrong with this entire setup and he planned to find out what was going on, whether Brac hired him or not. It would be easier if Brac thought Raj worked for him.

"Raj, it is nice to meet you. I have heard many good things about you. It is said you are one of the most successful Hunters, and I need the best. My daughter disappeared from our home six *bi-nons* ago and I fear for her safety."

Brac's tone of voice was correct, but as Raj silently studied him, he wondered at the sense of coldness emanating from the man as he related the circumstances of his daughter's disappearance. Brac managed to say the right words but the emotions didn't match.

"So, can you tell me what happened? Or at least what you know?"

"She had been swimming in our underground pond when she just...vanished. Alma, her watcher, was with her. The old woman fell asleep and has been punished for failing her duty. We don't know how my daughter left, where she went or why, but she must be brought home. Surely you can see the danger she faces if one of my political enemies captures her and tries to use her against me? Your job is to find her and bring her back to us."

Raj flinched at the man's callous attitude when he said he'd punished the watcher. His recitation also raised some interesting questions. Just whom did Brac think his political enemies were that they would take advantage of a young girl? Mica and Tar? *Ridiculous.*

"Does your Life Companion have any idea where she would have gone? May I talk to her?" Raj asked.

Anger radiated from Brac. "No," he stated flatly. "Zabeth is upset by this and I have given her something to calm her down. There is no reason for you to discuss this matter with my mate."

Okay...

"You say she has been gone...by the way, what did you say your daughter's name was?"

"I didn't," Brac snapped. "But her name is Ahnika and I told you she has been gone for six *bi-nons.*"

Interesting. Brac was barely controlling a deep rage. If he thought Raj would back off on the questions, he had the wrong man. "Is there a reason you waited almost a *non* to enlist the services of a Hunter?"

Brac sputtered and visibly made the attempt to calm himself. "For the first few *bi-nons*, I thought she would come back by herself or my people would find her. When neither of those things happened, I began to search for the best Hunter on Zylar. That took a little time. Plus, well...something you will need to be aware of, but I wouldn't want to be common knowledge — Ahnika can be a little *unstable* at times and is often melodramatic. I would ask that you not listen to her fantasies. I can give you a calming potion to administer as soon as you recover her. Having her unable to resist will make the journey back to Tanar easier on both of you."

Brac's unemotional pronouncement of the girl's *instability* caused Raj's eyebrows to rise. A father volunteering to send him with drugs to keep his daughter quiet opened up some very interesting questions. Questions he wouldn't ask. He'd rather see what happened when he found the girl.

"Okay, let's see what I can do for you. Do you have a holo-picture of her? No? Then please give me a description of your daughter."

Brac gave a brief, suspiciously impassive and completely worthless description of Ahnika. "I have no holo but I can describe her for you. She is short for a Zylan, about five foot and seven inches tall. She is twenty-one life cycles old. Her figure is curvy and she has brown hair that goes to the top of her hips." Once again there were none of the loving details a father would usually give about a daughter. No emotion showed, other than a tremendous anger over her disappearance. He reflected no deep concern.

"What color are her eyes?" Raj struggled to keep his own emotions under control and to show no reaction to Brac's statements. Was he being unfair, did his distaste for the man color his perceptions? Probably not, but striking out in anger at Brac's unfeeling attitude would get him taken off the job.

Brac hesitated, and thought carefully for a *minon* before answering, "Her eyes are hazel-colored and her skin is light red," he finally stated.

Interesting. Raj noted that it was obviously not a close family if the father couldn't immediately remember his daughter's eye color. He wondered at her skin coloring, Brac's was a pasty white. Maybe his Life Companion had the red skin tone or, perhaps, Ahnika was adopted.

The man was lying about something...probably several things. Raj sensed the deceit settle around him, coating the air with its black feel until he could almost taste the untruths. It was clear Brac hadn't researched Raj's talents. If he had, he would have known that, besides Hunter abilities, Raj was able to detect dishonesty. Raj chastised himself for not looking into Brac's past in more depth. Raj hadn't done enough preliminary investigation on this job. He couldn't tell in specific detail what Brac was being dishonest about, he couldn't divine the truth, but almost every word coming out of his mouth was tainted with lies. *What is going on in this place?*

I may be the best Hunter on Zylar, Raj thought to himself, *but I'll bet no one told Brac that I'm also the most ethical.* He often offered his services at no charge, simply in a need to help people. Just as there had been times when he'd refused a mission and the individuals would cry out in supplication and he'd hear them in his sleep. So he ended up helping them anyway. Raj knew his ties to this girl, Ahnika, were already formed, no matter what the father said. The battery of negativity and helplessness surrounding Brac's home, the shadowed hint of deceit and unanswered questions, ensured his involvement. He was going to help her — it just may not be in the way Brac wanted or imagined it would be. If the girl had a compelling reason for leaving, he would find her and, instead of bringing her back to her father, he would make sure she was able to stay out of his reach.

"I'll need to go to where she was last seen. When tracking someone, it is imperative I start from the last place the person was known to be. Will you take me to the bathing pool from where she disappeared?"

"Is that really necessary?"

"It depends on how quickly you want me to find her." Brac was clearly unhappy with this request and Raj was having a hard time pretending he believed even a small portion of the man's story.

After several minutes of scowling contemplation, Brac reluctantly agreed to allow Raj to be taken to the underground bathing pool where the girl had supposedly been swimming. Raj wasn't, however, allowed to go alone.

Obvious about his desire to be finished with the discussion, Brac didn't go with him but instead summoned the girl's watcher and a male guard to accompany Raj. Brac's attitude and actions continued to be very suspicious. *Why would a woman of twenty-one life cycles need a watcher?* Watchers were little more than babysitters, meant to control the antics of Zylan young. Raj was firmly convinced that something was terribly wrong and he suspected that there was more — much more — to come. None of it good.

Alma, the old watcher, shuffled into the room and without saying a word, she led him downstairs to an underground lake. The faded bruises on the old woman's face irritated Raj. If this is the way Brac punished one of his servants, then the action only added to his growing conclusion that this wasn't a simple case of finding a missing daughter. *But what else could it be?* The entire situation confused him and the presence of the burly guard made asking questions impossible unless he wanted every word to get back to Brac. Raj kept his silence.

As he descended into the tunnel leading to the bathing pool, he felt as if he were moving closer to the fortress' secrets. A barrage of depressing emotions hit him like the solid slap of a psychic hand from a side corridor, making his insides churn and his mind fill with fear. Fear that wasn't his. He tried to turn into the passageway but was quickly blocked by the appearance of two strongly built guards. Mean-looking specimens, their faces set on permanent scowl. "Leave." The curtness of their tone and hands going to flash wands at their sides ensured the message was clear. Raj would not be allowed access. Their show of force added to his suspicions. As if he needed anything else.

The glance he stole into the corridor produced a sudden fog enshrouded vision of a woman. She was holding her hands out to him, beseeching him to help her. Her long hair flew around her as if moved by an unseen wind, he could see tears in her eyes and dark bruises on her face. Beyond the colorless shadow despondency rolled and Raj stretched his senses, seeking...and then shook his head in disgust as he was turned from the corridor. The fleeting look raised the hair on the back of his neck. He'd seen several heavily barred doors lining each side of the hall. *It looks like a prison*, Raj thought.

He couldn't break the dampening shields that kept him from *seeing* what or who was down the corridor, but he knew in his soul that Ahnika wasn't here. The vision could only be part of the tie that often occurred between Raj and the people he tracked, allowing him to sense past hurts and present danger for those he sought. The secrets of Ahnika's past would have to wait. He needed to find her first.

Fighting Brac's guards would result in Raj being taken off the mission and Ahnika and her needs were more important. He reluctantly allowed himself to be led away by the guard sent to take him to the pool.

When they reached the underground cavern with the bathing pool, Alma explained, with the fewest words possible, how Ahnika must have passed by her while she'd slept against the wall. Alma believed Ahnika went up the stairs and into the house.

Raj didn't think so. When he asked for something of Ahnika's to hold, the elderly woman appeared confused and she was hesitant to provide anything until she'd cleared it with her employer. After she returned from conferring with Brac, Raj was given a small piece of old, worn clothing.

With downcast eyes, Alma explained, "This comes from one of Ahnika's favorite dresses." Raj got the psychic impression from the rag in his hands that it had been her *only* dress. *And how did* that *make sense?* Supposedly she was a member of this family—a very wealthy and prestigious family. Once again he shrugged off his growing anger and dread, knowing he would be of no help to the girl if he upset these people. He closed his eyes to see if he could feel her soul and pick up even the slightest trail.

At an early age, Raj had developed the ability to trace the sparkling essence of energy left behind when a person was in motion. These soul trails were linked to a person's aura but yet remained separate entities. He didn't understand all the nuances of his power and his brother and the Selven High Priestess had never heard of anyone being able to see such a unique and personal marking. When he'd discovered he could find missing persons with this ability, he became a Hunter.

Raj still spent many *nilts* with Zylan elders trying to explore the limits of his powers. Neither he nor anyone else had yet to figure out if there was more to the distinctive skill than its use as a tracking method. As Zylar's only soul tracker, any information on the soul trails came from trial and error when he followed or tried to use them. He only used this ability while tracking. Otherwise his vision filled with layers of multicolored ribbon. Becoming lost in the tangled patterns of people's lives, he would be oblivious to the world around him and its dangers.

Some soul lines were vibrant, cheerful. Some—dark and malevolent and he would have to block their effect on his own personality, as the murky tendrils seemed to shadow anyone around them. But the strands were always different, completely individual and a true reflection of a person's character. Raj believed his talent for sensing lies and deceit came from a sort of psychic resonance coming from the soul trails.

Regardless of what they were, Raj could trace them back to their owner. Once he isolated soul trails and identified the person it belonged to, he could recognize and follow it anywhere. No two were alike.

When Raj focused on calling Ahnika's soul trails to the forefront of his consciousness, he got more than he bargained for. He was swamped with sensations pouring into him from the cloth he held, the depth of the girl's unhappiness, her absolute terror and pain and the fierce determination to escape—all hammered into his mind.

Gradually, her soul trails appeared as a vibrant twisting tangle of blues and reds leading straight into the water and, he noted, it disappeared under a rock at the back of the cavern. There was no reemergence of the colors. The missing girl had either gone under the water to her death or there was a way out under the rock.

Ahnika's soul tendrils were devastatingly different from others he'd tracked. They seemed to reach out to him, as if trying to merge with his own aura. Raj had to psychically turn the threads away from his body. Never before had the tendrils of another's soul tried to touch him.

As his vision centered on her trail, one thing became very clear, she wasn't dead or the soul trails wouldn't— couldn't—be this electric. He'd wondered if an explanation for Brac's attitude could have been a cover-up of sorts. It wouldn't have been the first time he'd been hired to find someone who'd died under suspicious circumstances or who'd been killed. People seemed to think if they hired a Hunter to look for a missing person, the blame couldn't be laid on their shoulders when the body was found.

Now that he had the color and vibrancy of her life force in his mind and her general direction, he would be able to find her. All the impressions he'd received, plus the feelings he'd picked up from the cloth, kept him silent, kept him from saying anything to the old watcher.

Taking the small piece of clothing, Raj left the depressing influence of Brac's home. Usually, he asked more questions about someone he was trying to find. But he felt the answers given here wouldn't help in either his search for the girl or in his understanding the reasons for her fleeing. And she had left under her own power. Her soul trails were the only ones going under the rock—if someone had taken her, there would be additional threads heading in the same direction.

Moving along the general route the soul tendril had been headed, he followed the whispers of color which seemed to cling and tease his mind, far into the hills and overland to an outside lake. He could only speculate how this path must follow an underground river. At a small lake's edge, out from the bank about five feet, the tendrils of Ahnika's soul appeared luminously on top of the water. The hidden river had obviously dumped her into the lake.

Brac said Ahnika was ahead of him by over six moon risings. If he was telling the truth, her trail should have a faded and wispy look. Instead, the tendrils were fresh, bright. Considering possible explanations for their vibrancy, Raj wondered if Brac had lied about how long she'd been gone. The only time he could see soul trails this clearly after a full *non* had passed was when he tracked the whereabouts of his parents or his brother. People he had strong connections to.

Was he tied in some way to Ahnika as he was bound to his family? *Shivet!* This wasn't the first time he regretted so little was known about his abilities. Raj was never comfortable when new effects of his talent manifested.

It wouldn't surprise him to discover Brac had lied, but he would have thought the man would tell him she'd been gone for less time than she really had. Raj expected to discover the girl had been missing several times what Brac stated. The sharp, clear trail might be an indication of just the opposite. Brac could have exaggerated and she'd only been missing for a few short *bi-nons*. If so, the exaggeration added to an already complex puzzle.

As he'd been lost in thought, the vaporous red and blue strands moved, reaching out for him. When he noticed what the soul trails were doing, he rolled his eyes. Great. Another mystery to solve concerning Ahnika's colored tendrils. What were they doing?

Since he'd never encountered this phenomenon before and the remote area provided some privacy and seclusion, he decided to stand and let them come to him, to find out what the seeking threads would do. Watching as they slowly inched closer, he tried to objectively list his body's increasing awareness of their progress. His skin flushed hot and crawled with sensation. Pleasant sensation. He groaned as the ethereal ribbons reached out to touch his body. It felt as if a million light hands stroked over his flesh with velvet fingers.

He began to pant. *By the moons...what is happening to me?* His cock jerked and grew with just a stroke of Ahnika's lively essence. He watched as the diaphanous cords hovered over him and seemed to seep through his clothing. He could feel them circle his straining shaft and he felt a tight, heated suction...

"Stop!" Raj cried out in panic as he threw up a psychic block against the onslaught of sensation. He could not allow his mind to play tricks on him. Raj did not want to speculate on why the soul trails might be sexually connected to him. He would not jump to conclusions. Yet. The unusual reaction made him even more determined than ever to find Ahnika.

He would not allow the tendrils to have power over him. Stripping his clothes off with a thought, he dove into the cold lake to douse his unexpected arousal, all the while swearing to himself that he wouldn't let the sexual excitement detract from his mission. He would bring his body under control and find Ahnika. This wouldn't be accomplished if he just stood and — *what?* Let some woman's aura seduce him? The notion was ridiculous.

A few *minons* later, he'd redressed and started walking down the path refusing to replay in his mind the sensual teasing he'd just experienced. Resuming the hunt and using his innate abilities, it was easy for him to follow the pulsing blue and red strands to a small village near the water's edge.

The wisp of her trail could be seen weaving around the huts in the village and ultimately showed her going toward the forest, all traces disappearing into the dense trees. Unable to stop himself from worrying about how she'd get dry clothes and food, now he felt confident she'd been able to clothe herself and find enough provisions to sustain her for a few *bi-nons*.

He didn't want to alert the villagers that someone had been in their midst if they didn't already know, as they could carry stories back to Brac. It looked as if Ahnika's tracks headed away from Tanar and he could think of only two options in their direction. She might be going to the Selven Refuge to take sanctuary with the goddesses or she could be traveling farther into the northern mountains.

Chapter Three

** හ**

Ahnika felt giddy with her good fortune. When she left the lake behind her, she discovered a small village a short distance away. Cold and tired, she'd still been overjoyed to be able to make it this far.

Stealthily, she went into one of the small houses and helped herself to what looked like discarded clothing and some food. Taking only a little from each of several houses so there would be little chance of something being missed, she worked quietly and efficiently to gather the supplies she might need to survive for several *bi-nons* in the mountains. It was so late in the evening, the people were sleeping and she kept to the night's shadows. Ahnika's heart seemed to beat so loudly in her chest she feared she would be caught, but somehow she managed to evade detection and she sent a quick prayer of thanks to the Goddess.

Regretting the necessity for stealing food, clothing and blankets from these villagers, she knew there was nothing else she could do, as she had nothing to barter with or to leave in payment. Even if she did, she couldn't take the chance someone would discover her presence and pick up her trail. Her captors would send someone to look for her and she was hoping they wouldn't want to advertise her disappearance. If they did, it might give away their illegal and immoral activities.

However, she couldn't count on their need for secrecy. If Zylan royalty were involved, they probably wouldn't care if anyone discovered their horrid actions.

Making a promise to herself to return in the future and repay their unknown kindness, she slipped out of the village dressed and looking forward to a night spent outside rock walls.

For the next three moonrises, she walked until she couldn't take another step. She hoped traveling this way would reduce the risk of seeing and being seen by other travelers and the shadows would conceal her passage. She passed the time comparing Zylar to her home planet, Zmar. On both worlds, water flowed in varying shades of purple, the grass rose in multiple tones of blue and many of the trees were turquoise. The biggest difference between the two planets was the amount of land on Zylar and the fact that a great deal of it appeared to be unpopulated. There was so much space on Zylar left wild and unclaimed.

The heat radiating from Zylar's two suns drained her energy and drove her to seek deep shade while they were in the sky. Zmar only had one, but Ahnika was sure her sensitivity to the burning rays had more to do with her recent confinement. Zylar's three moons bathed the night with a wonderful silvery light that was far brighter than the one moon of Zmar. Unless clouds covered one or more of the moons, the night was almost as light as suns rise. It pained her to remember how much she'd wanted to spend time under these moons. Well...now she just wanted to go back to Zmar.

Thinking of home brought her thoughts to her family. Wondering how they were doing, and if they continued to search for her, hurt her deeply. She couldn't help praying her brothers and Janey had escaped the raiders. As tears filled her eyes and her steps slowed, she pushed the unhappy thoughts firmly away. The only thing she could do was get somewhere safe, and then find a way to contact her parents. Until then, she needed all of her emotional strength just to survive.

Hiding in a cave or under bushes, she slept under the light of the suns. On the fourth moonrise, she woke suddenly to find three women standing around her hiding place. Obviously, she wasn't hidden well enough.

Ahnika scrambled to her feet. "Who are you? What do you want?" She winced at the demanding tone of her voice when it seemed to reverberate with the fear she couldn't conceal.

One of the women stepped slightly forward. She was older than the other two and Ahnika estimated her to be about the same age as her own mother. Dressed simply in traditional men's clothing of a gray tunic and black pants, her dark hair was braided and hung midway down her back. She had kind, dark green eyes that lessened the otherwise blunt features of her face. As if she were afraid to upset Ahnika, the woman spoke softly, "We will not harm you, child. We ask only if you need our assistance. Are you well?"

Ahnika studied her and the others carefully. They didn't appear threatening in any way, but she had to be careful. "I am fine, thank you. Are you from a nearby village?" She winced, knowing she still couldn't manage to keep the panic from her voice. It had been so long since she'd spoken to anyone, she had lost the ability to conceal her emotions from her words.

"Yes," the woman replied. "Our village is near and you are welcome to come and stay with us for a time. My name is Anala and I am the leader in our community."

Before she could think, Ahnika was shaking her head. *No.* She hadn't run far enough, she couldn't chance—

"You will be safe, child. I promise you this. I am a seer and I know you will not be with us long, but you *will* be able to rest for the journey ahead of you. Our village, Jandai, is one of women and we would be happy to shield you from your troubles for a short time."

Ahnika's eyes snapped to Anala's. "A village of women?" She didn't question what the seer had seen of her troubles or the time she would spend with them. Ahnika didn't want to discuss it.

"Yes. No man lives in our village. We have chosen this life for our own reasons and you are welcome to take shelter within its walls. We don't need your secrets, child. Tell us what you would be called and come join us for the night's meal," Anala requested.

Ahnika debated with herself. Could she risk spending even a short time with these women? It eased her mind to know there were no men in the village. She wanted to ask *why* there weren't any but realized if she didn't want to share her secrets that she couldn't very well demand to know theirs.

They weren't pushing her. There wasn't much of a choice, she was out of food and needed to replenish her supplies. She could take the opportunity to rest a little and plan what to do next. Deciding not to use her own name, she instead chose her mother's in the hopes that when someone used it, she would pay attention and answer. If her captors found the village and asked for her, the change in name would hopefully provide some protection for the villagers as well as for her. "Call me Namilla," she said. "And I would appreciate the chance to rest with you for a few *bi-nons.*"

Nothing more was said. The women seemed content to leave her to her thoughts. They asked no questions and said little else as they helped her to gather her few belongings and escort her the short distance to the village.

Her skin color wasn't a curiosity as there were many varied flesh tones among the women. This was the first time she'd been given the opportunity to observe the diversity of Zylar's people her father had described. Once again the memory of her family made her falter, she pushed the sadness aside to concentrate on her surroundings.

The sight greeting her as they came out of the forest was a very small and almost primitive village made up of ten simply made wooden huts. The aqua tone of the wood created a vibrant picture in the moonlight. Ahnika noticed several women moving around the small rock-walled compound. But she saw no men and there were no children. It was a very quiet and seemingly peaceful setting.

Anala stopped in front of one of the houses and turned to speak to her, "Namilla, you will find a bed in this home with Tilana." Anala nodded at the tall, pale green woman with light blue hair. "We share our homes in groups of three or four. Tilana's housemates are currently away on a gathering trip so there is plenty of room for you to be comfortable. She will show you where you can bathe and will bring you to the communal house for something to eat. If you have any needs, just let Tilana know and we will try to take care of them."

* * * * *

After a few *bi-nons* of rest, sunshine and good food, Ahnika felt as if she'd been reborn. Still hyper-alert, she kept a bag packed and close to her at all times, just in case she needed to run. As she sat in the shade of a moonflower tree contemplating what to do next, she decided she couldn't stay in Jandai much longer. This time of healing was coming to an end.

She sensed a change in the air. After being kidnapped and brought to this planet, she had been kept underground and away from the moons' power. But with her freedom, came exposure to their influence and the possibility that whatever psychic gifts she might have would increase with her recent exposure to Zylar's moons.

Many psychic gifts appeared at maturity but she knew Zylar's three moons enhanced psi abilities. She didn't know the first thing about testing what was happening to her or how to develop what seemed to be an increased awareness. Anala might be able to tell her of exercises she could do to uncover them, but then she might ask questions Ahnika didn't want to answer. Maybe when she was home and safe, she would get a chance to experiment.

She could feel pressure against her skin, the sensation reminding her of a dark cloud moving toward her. Since she couldn't use her abilities to narrow down what that meant, she would take it as a hint to leave. The last time she ignored this impression, she'd been kidnapped from her home...she was not about to repeat *that* situation.

It didn't help that she'd also started feeling nervous around the women. They all seemed nice, but she could feel undercurrents in the village she didn't understand. There had been several times when conversations had ended when she joined a group of the women. Or maybe she should say arguments instead of conversations?

It almost felt as if there were a hint of fanaticism in some of this group. To a lesser degree, she recognized the same sort of psychic taint that had come from her captor. Sighing heavily in disgust, she shrugged her shoulders. It would have been nice if she could really be safe here. She didn't exactly feel danger coming from the women, just a strong intuition she didn't belong in this place. Unsettled and wary, she felt she needed to move on.

Hearing women's voices coming in her direction, she started to call out when the words of their conversation stopped her.

"I can see this path you wish to take bringing danger to us, Syblia. You need to rethink your plans." Anala was talking to one of the women who had just returned from the gathering trip. Ahnika had felt her discomfort increase since the women returned this last *bi-non*. What was the danger they spoke of?

"Anala, you are getting old and you are past the age of bearing children. You know none of us will ever link—Brac took care of that when he captured and tortured us many life cycles ago. After escaping from him, our bodies have healed but our minds never will. We will have no men in our lives…yet some of us want children. The potion will help us conceive. It will enhance our reproductive system so a link bond isn't necessary to the creation of life. But we still need a man's seed. We *will* eventually find travelers who stray to close to our village. We are hidden, but if Namilla stumbled upon us, others will. If they don't come to us, I can take other trips to find men elsewhere. When we have the opportunity, we will capture and hold any men we find and use them for their semen. All you need do is to strip them of their memory when we're finished. If you will not do this, we will kill them so our village can remain safe."

"Doing this, you will become the very thing we ran from. Brac tried to turn us into sexual slaves, taking our freedom and our choices. Now you would do this to others?" Anala sounded furious. "How can you even think of taking a man's seed, then killing him or tampering with his memories? You know trying to erase their time here could damage their minds beyond healing. I do not understand you, Syblia."

"Those of us who want more, who want children, are owed this," Syblia spat. "We've had too much taken from us. We're not willing to sacrifice *this* opportunity."

"Then go to a larger village, use the potion and entice a man. You do not need to kidnap one and tamper with their minds."

"Anala, you know there is no way on Zylar's moons we would allow a man to touch us or use us in any way. We will control this. We have prepared the cave for our captives. When any man comes to this village, we *will* bind them and take what we wish."

Anala and Syblia moved away. Ahnika could no longer hear them, but she was shocked and heartsick at Syblia's plans. No one deserved to be held against his or her will and used in such a way. Even if they were to hold this Brac, who Ahnika was sure had to be the same man that had captured her. *Brac.* She now had a name to put to the monster's face. Ahnika frowned. She hadn't paid a lot of attention to her father's meetings, but she was almost certain she'd heard him mention a man named Brac before.

Right now who he was didn't matter, Ahnika knew she wanted absolutely no part of this village if they would recreate the horror she'd lived through. She would leave in the morning.

* * * * *

Raj pursued Ahnika's psychic thread up into the wilds of the northern mountains.

This was an unsettled region and, as far as he knew, there were no villages or settlements for the girl to get supplies. Worried for her, he wondered if she found enough food or if she was able to keep warm during the cooler nights. His senses told him he was getting closer to her, but she remained just out of his reach.

Several *bi-nons* into his search, he stood on a high ridge and looked down, amazed to have found a small community well-hidden in the middle of a thick forest. If Ahnika's soul tendrils hadn't led him directly to the tiny village, he would never have seen it.

Raj was tired. He'd used up a great deal of energy just keeping those Goddess cursed tendrils from reaching out to him again. And he'd been using even more psychic energy trying to soul-shift at night—not one of his stronger talents—draining his life's essence by mentally going back to Brac's compound to see if he could, somehow, gather more information. Unfortunately, each soul-shift had been like hitting a brick wall. Brac's home remained tightly shielded and Raj hadn't been able to discover a way in, nor had the shields loosened enough for him to catch so much as a glimpse inside.

All he'd managed to accomplish with those nightly visits was to exhaust his psychic powers. He would soon need to find some willing female bodies to replenish his depleted strength.

Maybe he would find someone in this village. He watched the small group for this suns' rising and noticed how Ahnika's winding blue and red soul trails were woven all through the village tapestry. It appeared she'd spent some time here, although it looked as if she'd recently moved on. He could follow a very new tendril as it snaked out from behind the village and disappeared into the forest on the other side with no returning thread.

Raj didn't have the vitality he needed to follow her. It was too far to any other settlement to take a chance without feeding. He would have to see if he could find what he needed among these women before he could go any further. Both physically and psychically tired, he settled down to rest and before he could think clearly, he relaxed...allowing his shields to drop.

Within *minons*, he could feel the first touch of Ahnika's soul trails. Groaning, he realized he had no energy reserve to fight what was to come. From beneath heavy lids, he watched the pulsing red and blue fingers move over his body, creating the sensation of fingers running through his hair, caressing his face.

Slowly the ribbons moved over his arms and chest. In breathless anticipation, he watched a mist of purple color pool over his groin and teasingly hover in place. A light sheen of sweat coated his body and he shifted uncomfortably. His mind raced as he tried to work through his options, he had a choice. He could deny this experience and try to put his shields back in place, which would use the last of his dwindling psychic energy and leave him powerless against more danger than the soul trails. Or, he could see what the psychic ribbons would do to him. The first brush of pleasure tempted him. He could feel the clear, fresh essence of Ahnika's energy reach out and enclose him in its warmth.

Decision made, he relaxed in his hidden tangle of underbrush, surrendering to the phantom touch. With his capitulation, the ghost tendrils jumped him.

They caressed and skimmed over every inch of his covered skin. Pulsed. Raj shuddered with indrawn breath, as the mist simultaneously gathered between his thighs and hovered over his cock. Having clothes deadened the effect, so with a wave of his hand, he removed the barrier of fabric. And the entwined soul trails settled over him. Reached out to circle his nipples. Groaning softly at the moist suction running from his breast to his groin, he watched the bolts of red and blue energy spike and shimmer along the length of his shaft.

Feeling swollen and needy as the blood in his body surged and throbbed to the soul trails' tempo, he disbelievingly noted the colors dancing and playing over his skin, as they flayed his body with the most amazing sensations. The energy beat over him, alternating between a slightly soothing feeling and a tormenting fiery pleasure. The blue soothed, the red tormented…a rainbow of ecstasy held just out of his reach. Bending his knees, he dug his feet into the ground and pumped his hips. Struggling to find release, he forgot he wouldn't feel a welcoming cradle for his cock and that the expenditure would cost him needed vitality.

Waves of heated touch moved faster, swamping him as the curling swirls of energy drove his excitement higher. Soft fingers of sensual fire branded his flesh, making him arch into their caress, causing him to moan in rising need. The force stroking him began to pump and squeeze his cock. It pressed in on him and then slid along his thick length, searing him with vibrations so sharp he needed to fight for every breath.

The pulsing flares of heat grew firmer, faster, making him clench his muscles and grind furiously against the misty red and blue haze. In stunned distress, he felt his power build as if he were feeding from a woman's orgasm. The slight increase reminded him that he had to stop this now. He couldn't afford to let the needed energy dissipate with his discharge.

But he was powerless against the passionate embrace of the tendrils. For the first time in his life, he had no control. The colored bands of Ahnika's soul milked him and he felt the force of a thousand shockwaves crash over his body and a hot ejaculation of seed spurted and shot from the end of his cock in a climatic explosion.

Shivet! Raj groaned as his body underwent aftershocks as the soft tendrils slid from around his cock and off his flesh when he re-erected his shields. *What in the Goddess was that?* Just what he needed right now…to be completely drained with the very first orgasm since his training with the Selven when he was eighteen life cycles and learned that having such a release would require him a *non* of time to recover his energy. He wouldn't waste the effort it took to bemoan the fact that this climax had been a solo one.

Sitting up, he was amazed to find he wasn't weak, but actually felt a little better than before the onslaught of psychic sex. *Goddess!* This was going to take more thought than he was capable of at the *minon*. With a wave of his hand, he cleaned himself and redressed.

Needing to push away what just happened and concentrate on his next moves, Raj realized the interlude had given him a choice. With the little bit of added energy, he could continue to track Ahnika or he could go into the village and take the chance someone would be willing to feed his *Vampen* needs. He looked around him and sighed, he didn't think there were any other villages or towns within *bi-nons* of this place. Not understanding the nature of the energy he had just received, he still knew it wouldn't last long and he wasn't sure he wanted to chance using the tendrils again to gain the little bit of power the experience provided him. He would have to go into the village.

This small community perplexed him and made him nervous, he had yet to see one man or a single child and yet he counted about twenty-five women. The lack of men and children was odd. Not wanting to alarm the women any more than he had to, he decided he better see if he could get his needs met during the suns rise as he felt they wouldn't appreciate a stranger entering their village after nightfall.

With this thought, he strode from the tree line and made his way to the small arch in the stone wall signifying the village entrance. By the time he reached it, several women were gathered at the entryway.

At first, he was a little disconcerted when all the women stood and glared at him, they really didn't look welcoming. But Raj wasn't worried for long, he truly liked and enjoyed the opposite sex and women of all ages liked him in return. Never having met a female who could resist his caring, he was sure he'd be welcomed once they realized he posed no threat. He just hoped at least one of them would be unattached and interested in spending some time with him.

After a tall, dark-haired woman whispered a command, the women became more accepting and Raj relaxed. The villagers' reaction was most likely due to their isolation. He didn't imagine they got many visitors.

The tall woman approached him and spoke, "Sir, welcome to our little village. I am Syblia. We can see you are tired and dusty. Please come and share a cool drink with us and rest."

Raj smiled and accepted readily. "I am Raj and I thank you for your hospitality. I would appreciate something to quench my thirst other than the water I have had on my journey." This woman was nervous with him but he could understand her reaction if there really were no men in their village. Raj decided he would share a drink and light talk before he asked any questions about Ahnika or searched for volunteers.

While standing over the village and looking for traces of Ahnika's soul trails, he had seen overlapping tendrils of all the village inhabitants. Many of the women here had dark shadows within them, shadows that could mean a number of things. Attempting to mentally reach out and touch the women's minds to see if he could detect if the dark murkiness hid some sort of sickness...he also wanted to find if he could identify someone who would be receptive to having sex with him.

He was surprised to discover all the women's thoughts were blocked to him—an unusual event for a Hunter. Most of the time, he could read others with no trouble. First Brac blocked him from reading his mind and now these women were doing the same thing, the unusual situations were a little disconcerting. He hadn't realized how often he relied on reading at least the surface impressions of others. Maybe his psychic powers were draining more rapidly than he thought with his efforts to find the girl and trying to figure out what Brac was up to.

During his observation, he did notice a highly unusual and positive—for him—fact about this village—all the women were unclaimed and over the age of agreement. Thinking this strange, his need was so great he took it as a good sign and silenced his inner caution.

The women seemed to change their wary attitude toward him quickly enough and acted delighted with the idea of having a visitor. Syblia offered him what she said was a common Zylan restorative potion.

"Here, drink this and rest a *minon*. Then we would love to hear what brings you to Jandai." She handed him a simple mug of brew and he noted how this village seemed lost in past times, as if it had been tucked away for many life cycles. Their story would undoubtedly be very interesting.

The taste of the potion was bitter and Raj drank the liquid quickly. Thinking that they must not have a very well-trained herbalist, he was astonished to find himself rapidly losing consciousness. *They had drugged him!*

Nilts later, Raj woke to find himself naked and locked into arm and leg shackles in a cave. The women had him chained on his back on a low pallet, his feet spread apart and his arms tied together over his head. The metal restraints were fixed low to the floor, which left him spread-eagle with no way of using his body for leverage. A blanket had been thrown over his waist.

Furiously, he tested his bonds and tried to break them without success. He didn't have enough psychic or physical force left to fight this captivity, which left him completely helpless. He roared in anger, "What in the name of the Goddess is wrong with you people? Let me out of here!"

At his shout, several women moved into the chamber. "Good, you are awake." He recognized the speaker as the woman who called herself Syblia.

"What in the moons are you doing?" Raj demanded.

"You are our captive, we plan to use you for your seed, taking no pleasure from your body. Your role is to impregnate several of the villagers with children. There is no doubt a man with your...proportions will be very virile," Syblia informed him tonelessly.

"What are you talking about? Un-linked couples can't have children," he snorted in disgust.

"We have developed a potion which will enhance our ability to conceive without the mating bond," Syblia stated smugly.

"Well, it won't do you any good, I can..." Raj trailed off. No. He wouldn't tell them what he was. If he couldn't talk these psychotic women out of trying to use him, it could be his only way out. Raj tried to prepare mentally for what he must do.

Syblia didn't seem to notice his slip. "You just lay back and relax. Over the next few *bi-nons*, we will all take turns with you and then we will dump you in a village far from here. We can't allow you to retain any knowledge of us when you leave, so we'll have to alter your memories. Just do your job and an altered mind is the only harm that will be done to you."

He froze at this pronouncement. *They planned on altering his memories?* A chill ran down his spine, he knew mind-altering required a very skilled healer if it was to be done without causing some kind of permanent damage. He could be left completely brainless or with big holes in his psyche. There was no question he had to get out of here before they attempted to mess with his mind!

Syblia pulled the blanket off him and several women bent over him. He refused to look at them, to see them as individuals. Their hands and mouths moved over his flesh, touching everywhere on his body and he fought any response with a growing feeling of revulsion. This was not consensual and caring sex. This was a rape of his body and, possibly, his mind.

He had to get control of his emotions and turn this reprehensible situation to his advantage. Reminding himself there was only one chance of escape—as a *Vampen* he could use his very rare form of psychic talent to feed his mental strength and ability by feeding from the women's orgasmic release. His body took nourishment in the customary fashion, by eating food, but he fueled his extrasensory powers in an entirely different way.

When the women climaxed and dropped their psychic shielding he could feed from their energy and the more he fed, the more powerful and long-lasting his abilities became. Normally he took care of his needs with a carnal sharing, pleasuring women and taking great pride in his sensual prowess and the way he treated each and every one of his lovers. In return, the women knew he would use their energy to replenish his own.

These women were intent on taking his seed and using him against his consent…they would be very disappointed to find that, instead, he would be using them.

Over the years he'd honed his control, denying his body fulfillment in order to protect himself. If he were to climax with anyone but his link-mate, his power would be drained so low it would take *nons* to build up his psychic reserves to a level providing him enough power to do even the simplest things. Like concocting clothing with a thought.

Only when he found his Life Companion would he finally allow his body to seek release and spill his seed.

Linked with his life-mate, his orgasms would spiral and return to him — providing all the psychic energy he could ever need. Being *Vampen* meant having a climax at any other time could be life-threatening. He had been controlling his libido since reaching maturity. At thirty life cycles, he was literally incapable of reaching that point with anyone else. At this *minon* in time, he could only thank the Goddess that release was almost physically impossible. The thought of any of these women bearing his children made him ill.

These women would be frustrated and angry when they tried and failed with their plans. Raj grimaced as he remembered lying in the bushes outside the village. Well...he'd been incapable until Ahnika's soul tendrils seduced him. Shying away from the memory of his orgasm during the interlude in the hills with Ahnika's soul trails, he didn't understand what had happened then and thinking of it only made him want more. Now was not the time to lose sight of his current situation.

He had to turn his mind away from the realities of this...rape. Let them use him, and hopefully his expertise would force them into climax so he could feed. The thought disgusted him but he realized he had no choice.

The women worked relentlessly to get him hard, trying to prepare him for their use. It took Raj a great deal of time to control his revulsion, to shut off his mind and allow his body to quicken with lust. As soon as his cock got hard, Syblia lowered her body over him and he fought to keep his erection. She rode him hard, intent on getting him to spill while she worked to keep her own body from reacting.

Raj laughed bitterly to himself, she had chosen the wrong man for her plans. He knew how to lift, to rotate and move just right...it didn't take long before she was moaning in unwanted and fulfilled passion.

And he was left cold.

Syblia jumped off him in disgust and snapped instructions to the other women as she left to "cleanse his scent" from her body. Raj felt no empathy for her anger. He would do what needed to be done.

He was required to *service* several women that moonrise. Each time they climaxed and he didn't, they seemed to get more desperate. And angry. Not one of the women took pleasure in their orgasms. Instead they seemed to see them as a sign of failure.

They never realized their psychic energy and life force was pouring into him from *their* orgasms. His strength started to build and he waited impatiently for them to give up.

Raj shuddered. He loved women—he needed them to live, for Goddess' sake. He had never taken anyone by force or used potions or any compulsion over them. Sex had always been delightful, but this experience was a nightmare he couldn't have imagined. He never wanted to feel this way again. Dirty. Used. With no control over how his body was taken.

Clamping down on the depressing thoughts, Raj waited impatiently until he was left alone long enough to escape. Finally, the last of the women left and he could go. With well-fed psychic strength, Raj mentally undid his shackles, simultaneously cleaning the stench of forced sex from his body. As he walked from the cave, he clothed himself in soft, dark clothing. Though the night was fairly warm, he felt chilled to the bone. Adding a long cape, he tried to take some comfort from its enveloping covering. He wondered how long it would be before he again felt comfortable in his own skin.

The relief he experienced when he left the village behind and picked up Ahnika's trail just outside the walled courtyard in the forest, was enormous. Making sure to put plenty of distance between the bizarre villagers before he stopped to rest, he carefully covered both his mental and physical tracks, just in case the community had a female Hunter.

He was also careful to maintain a shield from the seeking threads of Ahnika's soul. Unwilling to share the degradation he felt, he knew it was crazy, but he didn't want the filth of the last few *nilts* to tarnish her.

Finally, when he'd walked until he could go no further, he stopped to rest and fell asleep under a tree.

The next suns rise, he woke up feeling very strange and dizzy. Trying to contact Mica, Raj couldn't seem to get his mind to work. He worried at first that he was sick from a side effect of the potion the women had given him, but this was something else...it didn't take long for him to realize he was extremely ill and needed help. He would have to delay his attempt to find Ahnika.

As he started for his home in the city of Zelph, at first he was able to move short distances with a thought or summon enough strength to transform into the dragon-looking *Peela*. This ability helped him close the distance he needed to travel.

As time wore on, he didn't have enough energy to stay in any form but his own. He'd almost made it to Zelph's boundaries when a band of thieves attacked him. Once they realized he didn't have anything of value, they took turns beating him and, in his current condition, he couldn't fight back. After they'd left him for dead, he managed to literally crawl the final distance to his home.

Chapter Four
A setnon later

ॐ

Raj strode through the majestic halls of the Selven Refuge having already stashed a few things in the room he used only for sleep and a little privacy whenever he visited. The High Priestess of the Selven stood at the end of the hall and called him to her. Shalan was an incredibly striking woman with long, very light blonde hair he'd never seen out of braids. Radiating power, she had eyes an intense violet shade and Raj knew if she wanted, those eyes would *see* entirely too much.

One of the strongest oracles on Zylar, if Shalan decided to delve into his mind and see what had happened while he'd been hunting Ahnika, she could do it easily. Nothing would be kept from her — not his misery at the hands of the women of Jandai, or his frustration in dealing with Ahnika's soul trails. After taking a *setnon* to heal from an insect bite while on his last hunt, he didn't have the strength to use any psychic shielding.

A fair and just leader of the Selven, Shalan had been chosen after the last High Priestess had kept Tar separated from his mate. Newly arrived on Zylar, Nyssa hadn't understood the ramifications of running from her link-mate after their bonding ceremony — but the previous High Priestess did, and she'd used Nyssa's lack of knowledge against them — hoping it would kill Tar and allow her to take over the throne. Shalan and several of the other goddesses had discovered her plans and helped to restrain her. The goddesses had then taken a vote and selected Shalan as their new leader on the strength of her compassion and her skills as a healer.

The Selven goddesses were women who had, for their own reasons, made the choice to never link with any male. Instead they went through a cleansing ceremony that physically removed the genetic triggers for the release of the mating links from their body. They trained and studied both psychic and healing arts and were responsible throughout many life cycles for the development of unknown psychic talents and dozens of medicinal cures.

These women lived as a communal group within the fortress called Selven Refuge, or, as it was commonly known, the gathering place. Raj smiled fondly and thought to himself, *a gathering place for exceptional women*.

The goddesses were freed from link bonding with any male, yet many of them gloried in unfettered sexuality. Their willingness definitely benefited him. Otherwise his *Vampen* nature and abilities would have been almost impossible to feed.

Many young Zylan males, before searching for their link mate, came to the Refuge to spend time with the Selven. Here they trained in the erotic arts. The practice had never been questioned, it was felt a man had a better chance of keeping his mate happy if he knew what he was doing. Raj grimaced. This rite of passage was likely to change if Tar's Earth-mate, Nyssa, or his own brother's wife, Tala, had anything to say about it.

And Nyssa and Tala had a veritable litany of *things* to say. Most of which started with sentences containing "Women's Rights" and segued into words like "equality for the sexes". Smiling, he realized the influence Nyssa had on their language. More and more Earth sayings were working themselves into Zylan speech.

Coming from Earth, Nyssa's view of how things should be caused sparks to fly around the ruling place. Tar's love for her and Nyssa's influence with her mate helped the Ruler see how the male-dominated society of Zylar affected women, and many of the antiquated laws and practices were changing. Nyssa had rammed the point home by mentioning that they would likely have a daughter some day, asking if Tar really wanted his daughter to grow up in a world were she was expected to do no more than keep her mate happy and bear his children. After an extended silence, his answer had been no.

The last conversation Raj participated in with the foursome had made his head hurt. Nyssa was very coldly informing her husband that she, as the Ruler of Zylar's mate, would be setting up a male equivalent to the Selven Refuge to "train" women in the erotic arts and how to use *their* links. Tala was adamantly supportive of the effort. Both Tar and Mica had looked dumbfounded and Raj left the room chuckling when the other men started to sputter.

The men's comments weren't making sense to *him* and he didn't have a mate. He certainly wouldn't want his Life Companion going to a male refuge to learn about sex. Nyssa would say he was a pig. Well, he didn't know what a pig was, but he knew when she called Tar one she hadn't been flattering.

But for this *bi-non*, unlinked men of all ages were welcomed at the Refuge. For him, their existence was a vital necessity. The Refuge was the only place where he could completely feed his *Vampen* requirements. The goddesses would stand in line for the opportunity to spend time with him and to assist in taking care of his every erotic requirement, allowing him the opportunity to enhance his psychic power when he fed.

Well, he was in the perfect place to give those abilities a much-needed boost. If getting lost in the sensations turned out to be harder than it used to be, too bad…he didn't have a choice until he found his mate. Raj gave himself a mental shake, he needed to step away from the memories and remind himself how he used to enjoy this. Well, *enjoy* wasn't exactly the word he would apply to this situation. *Thrived*…maybe. *Fed on it*…most definitely. But the women in Jandai had changed him.

Feeling sorry for his situation wouldn't feed his *Vampen* strength, nor would the realization that *this* time with the Selven, he would leave miserable and unsatisfied. Having only fed from—and not shared in—the passion, Raj knew until he found his mate, *Vampen* feeding would be more of a chore than a joy.

Shalan interrupted his thoughts. "Raj, how wonderful to see you doing so well." Such a beautiful man with wavy, dark brown hair and a well-formed muscular body that filled out his tunic and pants. His pale blue eyes seemed somewhat sad and preoccupied and she wondered if she should dip into his thoughts and see if she could do anything to help. Maybe he'd ask her for assistance. She hated prying without a specific need. "May I speak with you privately for a *minon*?"

"Sure, Shalan. What do you need?" As Raj replied he followed her through a door at the end of the hall.

Once they were behind closed doors in a small antechamber, Shalan turned to him. "Would you like something to eat or drink? I wanted to find out how you are feeling, Raj. I know Mica was very concerned with your health. Are you back to your normal energy reserves?"

Pushing his inner turmoil away, he smiled broadly and answered her, "Almost, Shalan. A couple of sessions with the goddesses and I will be at full power. You know I was completely drained after my illness. Thank Zylar's moons for

71

the Selven! If I didn't have your sanctuary and the women willing to help, it would take me a life cycle to feed this time. I don't need anything right now to eat or drink. I am impatient to get back to trying to locate the woman I was tracking when I became injured."

Shalan snorted. "Oh, believe me, the goddesses are more than willing to help. I will be lucky if I don't have to break up an argument or two while you are here...they are so willing. Which reminds me...I have something for you that may help with your energy. But first I wanted to ask you what made you so ill? Mica didn't go into any detail in the short time he was here claiming Tala and, as a healer, I am very interested in what happened to you. Can you tell me anything about what caused your illness?" Her light teasing only brought a slight smile to Raj's face. She sensed a change in Raj—in the past, this man had been all sensual light, happy to be here and raring to go. Now there was something different in his demeanor...something dark. It seemed almost as if he were dreading his time with them.

"Evidently I was bitten by a Zylan *Nej*. Have you heard of them, Shalan?"

Frowning and shaking her head, she asked, "No. What's a *Nej*?"

Raj remembered what one of the ancient healers had told Mica. "According to, Naja, the *Nej* is a spider-type insect long thought to be extinct. They have one fang and, if you are bitten, the venom it injects through this fang moves quickly through the bloodstream to your brain. From Mica's description, this venom somehow creates its own web and wraps the victim's mind up in a sort of cocoon. My bodily functions continued and while Mica thought I was unconscious, I still had some ability to understand what was going on around me. I could hear but couldn't react and I remember almost everything said and done to me. I think if

my body had been healthy instead of damaged
thieves' attack, I could have moved around. Bu
completely worn out and couldn't respond or move
way. I couldn't talk or lift a finger to do anything
myself. My mind was there, yet it was locked away fr
body, unable to make any connection to move or
When Toma would tell me to drink, I would try very
comply, but my injuries were just too severe. Naja is
Mica some old texts that might help him to look into the
history and see what he can find."

"Like the *Nubes*," she whispered in awe. *Could this
Could the answer to the Nubes' problems be as simple as an
bite?*

"Sorry, Shalan, I didn't catch what you said?"

"Nothing, Raj, it's not important right now. I will hav
talk to your brother in more detail about the *Nej*."

"Well, any chance he gets, Mica has been studying wl
he can find out about them, talking to all the ancients as we
I am sure he knows more about them now than he did whe
he healed me. Mica mentioned I didn't have any brai
activity that he could trace and I was so tired, I forgot to tel
him I knew what was going on around me. I need to
remember to tell him...it might be important," he replied
absently.

"I'll tell him as you will be hunting again soon and may
not have the opportunity. I think the fact you were aware of
your surroundings when you appeared comatose is very
important. I will also search our healing archives for any
mention of the *Nej*," Shalan offered.

"Great. I'd better go, Shalan. I need to get back on the
trail of my latest job, and I am not quite up to speed yet." His
response seemed halfhearted. Watching his mood change and
bewilderment replace his carefree grin, she wondered again

out what had happened to this man over the last *setnon*. Shalan, can I ask you a question?"

"Of course. What is it?" Raj looked uncomfortable and Shalan tried to decide what could be bothering him and if she should interfere. She didn't like to use her powers as seer to intrude on others emotions unless it was needed. Sighing she kept her mind blocked.

"I know how you've studied and tried to replicate my abilities with soul trails and I haven't talked with you in a while about your progress. Have you found anyone else who has this ability?"

"No. No one else has been able to see any more than a person's aura, and the person has to be right in front of them when they see even that much. We haven't had any luck replicating your gift. Why do you ask?"

"No reason. You'd let me know if you ever made any progress with this, right?"

"Absolutely, Raj. Has something happened?"

Raj frowned. "Not something I'm willing to share yet. Mostly because I am not sure what *is* happening. I will let you know if I find something out." Raj wasn't quite ready to share the experience he'd had with Ahnika's soul trails. It was just too personal.

Shalan shook her head in exasperation. Something was going on with him. But if he wouldn't confide in her, she couldn't pull the information out of him. Well…she *could*, but she would respect his privacy. She didn't spend too much time worrying about Raj as her thoughts were spiraling madly around the problem of the *Nubes* and whether the *Nej* could be the answer she'd been searching for.

The Selven had been in charge of the care of five *Nubes* for over a hundred life cycles. They were men who had no discernible mind or emotions and no one knew where they came from. Or what had happened to make them lifeless

shells. The five did nothing on their own—the Selven told them to eat, to drink, and to bathe. The *Nubes* didn't talk or react to any stimuli other than a direct order. Much of her life with the Selven had been spent trying to find a way to heal their minds and she felt driven to find a cure for them.

Even when she knew what she really wanted was a cure for *him*. The Golden One. A perfect shell of a man she'd lusted after and then cared for and protected for many life cycles. Sometimes she wondered if her life would ever feel complete until he could smile at her, talk to her. Sighing, she pushed the possibilities away for the *minon*. Raj's earlier comment about being up to speed broke through her thoughts. *The potion.*

Shaking her head in annoyance with herself, Shalan rolled her eyes. "I remember why I really wanted to talk to you. I know it can be dangerous for you while you are hunting if you deplete your psychic powers and are unable to find a woman to feed from. Not to mention the fact that one woman is rarely enough for you. I have been working on an herbal potion, one that should increase sensitivity and sexual response in your partner. I thought it would be useful to you, especially when you are away from the Selven. If you only have a single woman to feed from, this potion should increase the potency of her orgasms, allowing you to gain more power. It's taken me awhile, the problem has been finding the correct form...it couldn't be in a lotion, because you might be affected as well and it would hamper your innate *Vampen* abilities to control your response."

Thinking of how much control he would have to exert to be with several women at a time...never having his own climax, she paused. Shaking her head to stop that train of thought, she went on. "This tincture needs to be taken internally by each of your partners and I believe only a small amount will be sufficient. I haven't been able to think of a way to test it but, if you want, you can take the potion with you and see if some of the Selven will try it for you. The amount of psychic energy released from a single orgasm should be multiplied. In theory, it will only take a drop or two of the potion for each participant. There will be plenty left in this batch for you to take with you on this hunt. If it doesn't work…well, the ingredients won't harm anyone and I'll keep working to find something else to help you."

Raj was stunned. For the first time his smile reflected a shadow of the man he'd been. Looking at Shalan, he wondered if she knew what she had done for him. He would welcome *anything* that allowed him some respite from the multiple seductions he required. "Thank you, Shalan, I'd love to give it a try. It would definitely be handy while I am away from the resources here at the Refuge."

Shalan was taken aback by Raj's delight over her gift, she had never realized feeding his *Vampen* nature might be a chore for him. Shaking her head she turned down the hall mumbling under her breath, "Resources? More sex than most men could handle. Resources indeed."

* * * * *

Raj went to the group of willing goddesses waiting in the large chamber hall. He explained how he wanted to do an experiment and that he was looking for volunteers to help him try the new elixir Shalan had made for him. He chose three women who were more than willing to take the test. They had partnered him before and were aware of his special needs. The first volunteer, Natanala, was a small, dark-haired woman with very large breasts. The second woman was tall and muscular, her hair was very short and curly, and her name was Inat. The third woman, a favorite called Lania, was dark-skinned with beautiful blue, almond-shaped eyes and wavy black hair.

After entering a small private room, each goddess removed her clothing and knelt on the floor cushions. Raj shook the bottle and put drops of the clear potion on the tips of three of his fingers. One at a time, each goddess moved to lick the fragrant drops from a single digit.

Holding Lania in his arms and running his hands over her soft skin, Raj began kissing each of them in turn and caressing their bodies. Usually the soft variations of velvet skin would enthrall him and he could get lost for long *minons* in a woman's unique contours and flavors. This time he touched, but didn't feel. Kissed, but didn't taste.

He'd left his pants on and these three did not question his actions, they knew from prior experience that, occasionally, he didn't fully disrobe. When he was really drained, remaining covered kept him focused on nothing but the feeding. Having just spent a *setnon* healing from the *Nej*'s bite, he was as weak as he'd ever been. With the added psychological residual of still feeling used, circumstances induced him to choose goddesses who were familiar and known to be undemanding, he hoped feeding in this way would make the situation easier for him.

Soon all four of them were sprawled among the floor cushions, kissing, stroking, and licking their way along each other's bodies. Raj kissed and suckled Lania's breasts, he positioned her on her back on the cushions with Natanala and Inat lying in similar postures on either side of them. While his mouth worked over Lania's body, his hands similarly caressed a woman on each side.

Often when with the Selven, he would have them play and tease him, he would submit to and enjoy their ministrations as the goddesses leaned over him and ran their hands slowly along his sides and chest where they could fondle and tease his nipples. Eventually silken hands would slide down his body until they became entangled in the nest of hair surrounding his penis. With a talented few strokes, his erection would increase and pulse with life. He would enter them and enjoy the feeling of being surrounded by their orgasmic vibrations. But not this *bi-non*. Not…yet. He needed more time to heal from his experience in Jandai.

Moving slowly down Lania's body, he moved his mouth along her rib cage, playing with his tongue in the small dip of her belly button. His hands mimicked his actions on Natanala and Inat. Positioning his mouth over Lania's center, she helped him by moving her hands down to hold the folds of her labia open for him, exposing the hard nubbin and the sweet softness of her clit. She was already creaming for him. His fingers found the other women open and wet for him as well.

The women panted and groaned with their hips thrusting high in the air as he used his tongue and fingers to drive them to release. If his tongue stroked, his fingers did the same, if he nibbled Lania's hard little nubbin, he pinched the clits of Inat and Natanala. Raj went through the motions, knowing what reaction each trace of his lips or hands would elicit. He could feel the anticipation and sensual heat building in the small chamber, yet he held himself separate from the women and their responses.

Within only a few *minons*, he pushed the women over the edge and they exploded with fierce orgasms. Stretching over the mingled bodies, Raj bent to place his palms in contact with their heated flesh. Absorbing the energy from their mutual climaxes, as a sponge would absorb water, he became flooded with their psychic discharge.

Raj sat back on his heels and glanced around him. Realizing the women were completely drained and falling into sleep, he stood up and extended his muscular frame into a long stretch to work the kinks out of his lean body. It was done. The potion had worked. The psychic power released with the moans and shouts of satisfaction was—at the very least—quadrupled.

The experiment worked so well that Raj's psychic energy had been restored to a new level. Walking slowly to the door, leaving the slumbering goddesses without a backward glance, he knew it was time to resume the hunt for Ahnika.

He wanted to head for Tanar, the Ruling Place where his brother served as High Priest and spend time with his family. Mica and his new mate, Tala, were waiting for him to join them but he knew he needed to find Ahnika soon.

Raj shook his head. *Tala.* Who would have thought that the pesky little tagalong would end up linked to his brother? Mica had evidently known for many life cycles that she was his link mate, his Life Companion, and Tala had almost given up everything and joined the Selven goddesses when she couldn't imagine being linked with anyone but Mica. Their lack of communication had almost kept them separated for eternity.

His brush with death, while tracking Ahnika, had added to their problems.

Running his hands through his long, dark brown hair, Raj paused before opening the door to exit the chamber. Assessing his body and inner being, he couldn't believe how he was at full psychic ability after only one feeding. With a thought, he used some of that energy to cleanse the smell of sex from his body and changed his clothes as he opened the heavy door, grimacing when he saw another group of goddesses waiting for him. They were every size, shape and color imaginable.

The gathering place had always been a necessary haunt for him, the women knew what he needed and would willingly provide it and he didn't want to displease them. Linked women—women with a mate could not service him, as it was physically impossible for them to do so. Un-linked women outside the Refuge were generally off-limits for his needs as well—their fathers and brothers saw to that. There were very few unattached women outside the Refuge that he could feed from, and one had never been enough in the past.

But he would have to tell these goddesses that Shalan's potion had worked so well he wouldn't need them now. He'd let them down gently, without leaving hurt feelings, as there would always be a next time.

As a *Vampen* Hunter, not having psychic strength could mean his death. He always had to have enough time and enough women to build the reserve between assignments or he put his life at risk. Lately his needs left him feeling cold and lonelier than he'd thought possible. After this job was finished, he promised himself the necessary time and concentration to try and find his mate. He knew his brother would help him search, as Mica had helped Tar to find his Life Companion.

Shrugging his shoulders philosophically, he moved toward the waiting women. Might as well get it over with. His power was now fully charged and he could leave here.

While packing his belongings, he thought about this job. His Hunter psychic powers enabled him to track people or things by a slim psychic thread. Now that he was refreshed, he should be able to pick up Ahnika's trail fairly easily. He knew Brac hadn't waited for him to heal before hiring other Hunters. No, Brac had probably sent them out even before Raj was injured. Fearing the new Hunters would have little or no moral character, as many in his profession were little more than thieves or had reputations for brutality, he'd made a few subtle inquiries this *bi-non*, and been relieved to discover no one had been successful in locating the girl.

Raj prayed to the moons that he could find her before the new Hunters discovered her location. The trail would be cold…but not impossible.

It didn't take long to gather his few possessions, as one of his more developed psychic powers was the ability to call or create objects he needed. He would depart as soon as he told Shalan how extremely well her potion worked.

* * * * *

Ahnika knelt in the soil of the garden, oblivious to everything but the glaring heat of the suns and the feel of the rich dirt in her hands. She was pleased with her situation for the short term. She'd been able to remain free and none of the Hunters she'd sensed over the last *setnon* managed to get close to her.

Her awakening senses gave her plenty of warning and she'd known when someone was looking for her and easily coped with avoiding them. The only real fright had come when one Hunter got close and then lost her when she left JANDAI.

Funny...she almost always thought of the village in capital letters. She'd found shelter and protection with the women for a short time and she would always be grateful to them. But when she'd felt those vague whispers in her mind, she'd known it was her signal to move on. The last time she ignored those soft voices, she'd been taken from her home in Zmar. This time she refused to overlook their warning...even if she didn't understand everything they were trying to impart.

So she'd fled and, watching from a far hill, she'd seen the tall silhouette of a man as he'd walked toward the village. Thank the Goddess she'd listened that time.

Yes, she'd been glad of an excuse to leave. But she felt sorry for the unknown man. The women were ardently militant, a strange group of psychics and healers with a palatable hate of men. They had some severely scary plans to breed a bunch of children by capturing unwary men.

Ahnika shuddered, suddenly cold. She was really afraid they had already started. The Hunter who had been so close on her trail would have stumbled into the village unaware of their plans for any man they got their hands on.

Ahnika wasn't very happy with males right now either, but she was sane enough to realize she didn't hate all of them. She loved her father and brothers and hated the idea that someone would hurt another person as the women on Jandai planned.

As always, thinking of her family made her sad. She wanted to go home, back to her own planet and see if her family was still alive. They probably thought she was dead or lost to them forever and she didn't want them to worry for her. She wanted to see for herself if Janey and the boys were okay. *Don't worry...I've made it this far. I can do the rest*, she told herself.

Maybe even find her way home. She turned her thoughts away from the painful memories of Zmar and back to the task at hand. Gardening. And figuring out what to do next, she knew she couldn't stay here forever.

For now, she felt safe, well-hidden in the mountain city of Vidar. She enjoyed the cold at night and warmth during the suns rise in this high retreat. The small city was large enough to hide her and, because it served as a crossroads for many roadways, there were lots of strangers in the town...she was just one of many.

She'd been lucky to find an older couple who required someone to help take care of their home and garden in return for room and board. Working on blending and staying hidden, she'd survive until she could figure out how to get home.

Her *bi-nons* were spent doing housework, working in the garden or going to the market. She liked Nebet and Gardeil, the elders who had taken her in. She smiled as the woman,

Nebet, slowly walked toward her. Ahnika was kneeling in the garden weeding the small patch of land.

"Namilla, you work too hard. You should come in and have something cool to drink and rest while the two suns are at their peak."

"I am almost finished, Nebet. I would like to get this done as next *bi-non* I will be going to market. You know how those women like to haggle over every little thing and it will take me nearly all suns rise to make our purchases." Looking up, she grinned fondly at the petite woman, Nebet's hair was almost completely white and it was always piled on top of her head in a wispy bun. Ahnika hadn't asked the couple, but she realized they had to be well over two hundred life cycles old. A Zylan's hair didn't usually turn fully white until the person reached the two-century mark.

"You should definitely go into the house, Nebet. You know you tire quickly in this heat. I will join you in just a few *minons* once I have finished this small section."

"All right, you bossy little thing. I will let you work out in this hot sun while I go rest these old bones in the coolness of the house. I will send my mate out to fetch you, however, if you take overlong," Nebet told her in no uncertain terms.

Ahnika smiled and paused to watch Nebet as she walked slowly back to the little, dark green, five-roomed house she'd called home this *setnon*. The house had a common room with cooking, eating and gathering facilities, a bathing chamber, two sleeping chambers and an herbal room where Nebet mixed her healing potions.

Behind the main wooden structure was a small shed, also dark green, where Gardeil worked on his manuscripts. Books overflowed from the shed and littered the house. Ahnika spent many hours looking at the tomes Gardeil still painstakingly illustrated. He was currently working on updating the history of Zylar's Rulers. Ahnika poured over the writings and hadn't found anything that would make her think the Ruler, Tar, had been involved in her captivity.

When she casually mentioned the name Brac to Gardeil, saying she had heard his name in her travels, he frowned and told her that he knew little about the man. Gardeil only knew Brac as one of the Ruling Council of Ten and a Zylan traditionalist. When pressed, Gardeil did say he'd heard how Brac often argued with both the Ruler and the High Priest about the shifting status of women in Zylar. That revelation caused chills to run up and down Ahnika's spine.

Gardeil did know a lot about the Ruler. It seemed Tar had linked with an Earth woman and she'd caused quite a stir when she discovered women could use the companion links. The Earth woman made public statements about changing the status of women on Zylar and Brac was vehemently opposed to both her involvement and her plans.

Returning to her weeding, Ahnika contemplated the idea of Brac being the one to kidnap her. The women in Jandai had mentioned a man called Brac, and it sounded like their experience with him had been very similar to hers. He would have access to tunics bearing the ruling crest. She frowned. In fact, he could make up tunics of his own and she and her people wouldn't have known if they were legitimate or not.

It was definitely something to think about. If she truly felt Zylan royalty had nothing to do with her capture and didn't know what was being done to the women in the fortress...maybe she should go to the Ruler and tell him. Gardeil worked for the Ruler illustrating the histories and he could probably get her an audience.

Or she could talk to Tar's mate. After her kidnapping and the experience with those inhumane men, it would probably be easier for her to approach a female. She didn't think she could explain her ordeal to the Ruler.

It was something to think about.

Ahnika's head snapped up and her eyes glazed in a sort of trance. She felt a dark shadow move over her, searching...

Trouble was coming. Concentrating, she tried to focus on where the sensations might be coming from. Was it someone searching for her? Did the feeling stem from something else she knew nothing about? Cursing, she wished again that she had some way of knowing how to develop this growing power.

Ahnika needed to do something but the feeling of unease was too vague to be of any help. Frustrated, she closed her eyes and tried to open her mind to any internal suggestions but the whispers were silent. *Shivet!*

Considering her options, she decided once again she wouldn't take any chances. She refused to be a victim any longer. She couldn't stay hidden forever, unless — maybe — she wanted to go back to Jandai. No, she dismissed the unsavory option very quickly.

Instead, she would gather her courage and go to market tomorrow. Using the little money she'd earned working for her new friends, she would purchase a few provisions and another disguise.

Then she would talk to Gardeil and Nebet and tell them what had happened to her and see if they would give her a paper of introduction to the Ruler's mate.

This moons rise she would relax and rest, struggle to enjoy a final night of safety and normalcy before she started her dangerous trek. It would be impossible to guess what might happen to her along her journey to Tanar. She needed to be ready for anything.

Chapter Five

ॐ

Raj contemplated where he should go from here. Sitting outside Jandai, he was carefully hidden both physically and with full psychic shields in place, as he didn't want to take the chance of meeting any of the crazy women of this village ever again. Letting his thoughts roam as he mentally scanned the area, he found no trace of Ahnika's vibrant blue and red soul threads. He really hadn't thought she'd still be hanging around this area, nor did he think his powers would be strong enough to catch a trace of *setnon*-old soul trails. Jandai was just the last place he'd seen a trace of her, so it made sense it would be the best place to start.

This whole situation was strange and growing stranger. His brother hadn't heard of anyone missing and if it involved one of the Ruler's Council of Ten, Mica should have been told. In fact, Mica hadn't even known the councilor *had* a daughter.

After much discussion, Raj and Mica concluded it would be better not to alert Brac to their suspicions. They wouldn't question him, nor would they alert him to Raj's connections to Tar and Mica.

Raj realized he had no intention of taking the girl back to Brac. His plan now was to find her — not for Brac but because he knew with inner certainty she needed help. In fact, he had a hunch she was the woman who had been calling to him for help in his dreams. While he didn't recognize the dim outline of the woman, the aura surrounding his vision matched the colors in Ahnika's soul trails. And…the dreams were always the same.

Feeling a sense of sadness, of terror emanating from the woman before him, Raj became overwhelmed with the need to help her. The woman's long hair curtained her upper body and fell to the floor concealing thin arms bent to cradle her face in her hands. It was too dark to tell what color her hair was, or to see much beyond the slight figure kneeling on the stone floor. But he could tell she was crying, bent double and shaking with the force of her sobs in a cold, dark room reeking of fear. Struggling to get to her, he tried to ask her what was wrong and what he could do to help. But a thick, mental barrier kept him away from her. Kept his words from being heard. Some unseen entity held him back when he desperately wanted to help. His body fought to move to her side. He tried again to reach her. To call to her.

At this point he always woke up feeling frantic and afraid for the woman, his body drenched in a cold sweat and his heart pounding furiously. He knew intuitively that he needed to find the woman in his dreams — the woman he believed to be Ahnika. Time was running out.

Even more disturbing was the memory of Ahnika's soul trails bringing him to climax. It became progressively more difficult to ignore his recollection of the red and blue energy and the sweet release brought by those psychic tendrils. Wondering how she could do this to him and why she seemed to matter more than any of the others he'd helped over the many past life cycles...drove him crazy.

Raj's thoughts circled back to his present dilemma. Ahnika wasn't in or around this village and it made him nervous being close to this place. Where would she go? He picked up on the psychic impression of others out there, looking for her. These Hunters were a dark, somewhat heavy presence in the psychic fabric surrounding him. This meant, as he got closer, they would also be able to feel him, unless he shielded himself. Shielding would take psychic energy to maintain. Thank the Goddess for Shalan's potion!

This led him back to his original reflection. Where would a girl in hiding go from here? Not to any sparsely populated area because she'd be easily spotted. Since he hadn't caught a glimpse of her soul trails as he'd made his way back to this spot—and he would have if she'd gone toward Tanar, that really only left one other option.

Ahnika must have traveled closer to the mountain crossroads. There were always strangers moving through the area, on their way to the far lands and the inhabitants of this region wouldn't pay attention to one girl. Well, it was a plan. He would head up into the mountains toward Vidar. If he shifted to the form of a *Peela*, he could be there by the next suns' rise.

Picturing in his mind the shape and substance of a Zylan dragon, Raj shifted his physical form. The creature rose above the land, circled and headed for the mountain range in the distance. The *Peela's* wingspan spread over twenty feet and would allow him to cover great distances in a short period of time. Another advantage to this form was the *Peela's* eyesight, since with it, he would be able to distinguish soul trails from far above in either sunlight or night's darkness.

Covered in dark brown scales matching Raj's hair perfectly, the *Peela* expelled a gust of fire as the giant creature filled the late afternoon sky. In the dragon's form, Raj took perverse satisfaction from hearing the cries of fear coming from the women of Jandai below.

* * * * *

Early the next *bi-non*, Raj walked down the road leading to Vidar's main outdoor market. The small streets were crammed with colorful, fabric-draped booths and the wares on display appeared to be varied and plentiful. Food, metal goods, clothing and books filled the temporary shelves.

Unfortunately he wasn't the only Hunter in the marketplace, there were many others circulating through the crowds. Like him, they were searching for the girl. For Ahnika. Even though his skin crawled with the sensation of eyes passing over him, none of them would be looking for him, as he'd deliberately neglected to inform Brac he felt well enough to resume the hunt.

To disguise his long hair and muscular build, he'd dressed in an elder's light blue tunic and loose-fitting black pants and had added a floor-length drab gray robe with a hood. After shrouding himself with a psychic shield, Raj had confidently entered the bustling market knowing his presence would not be detected.

Raj knew all Hunters had an inherent ability to track...hence the choice of profession, but each Hunter's gifts and accomplishments varied greatly. His ability to see soul tendrils was unique and gave him an edge over the others.

Discreetly looking around the bazaar, he could feel and see many traces of Ahnika. Her tendrils ran through the market—some older, some more recent. The distinctively vibrant twist of blue and red signifying her proximity crisscrossed and ran haphazardly from place to place. It seemed Ahnika had, at one time or another, touched each and every booth in Vidar's busy public square. Once again, he was forced to fight against those filaments of her soul as they reached out to stroke along his skin.

A commotion near the end of the street drew his attention away from the mesmerizing draw of Ahnika's essence. A slight figure dressed in a costume similar to the one he wore, was being held captive between two very large and obviously irritated men. Raj sighed with disgust, it was just his luck to be a few *minons* too late to find and remove her without detection.

Ahnika's blue and red essence completely enveloped the small figure. On closer inspection, he recognized the two men. Jondil and Zaben. His eyebrows rose in contemplation. Brac's choice of Hunters for the girl had certainly bottomed out. These two were not known for their skill but for their willingness to take any job. Both men were utterly ruthless and were wanted for questioning about a death that had occurred during their last mission.

In fact, Tar had asked Raj to take on the chore of running these two to ground when his current job was completed. Unfortunately for Ahnika, both Jondil and Zaben were strong and well-trained in psychic battle. Raj wasn't pleased to have to deal with them together. Fighting both men and shifting the woman to another place would require a great deal of psychic power — almost all he had left.

Apologizing silently to Tar, he realized his first and only priority was to get Ahnika away from Jondil and Zaben. Once he'd assured himself of Ahnika's safety, it wouldn't be too difficult to locate and bring the two men in for questioning.

Watching them drag the woman down a side street and away from the market, he quickly moved to follow. Raj could feel additional Hunters in the area. Were they working on their own or were they helping these two? He needed to move while he had the chance. The odds — two against one — were bad enough but he didn't want to stick around and see if they'd get worse. Nor did Raj want to give the Hunters an opportunity to transport her some distance away with their psychic location shifting. He couldn't leave Ahnika unprotected and vulnerable to the brutality these two brutes often used against their prey — if they shifted with her, they'd be almost impossible to track.

* * * * *

Ahnika was frightened. Like a fool, she'd sensed the Hunters nearby but decided to take the chance her shielding and disguise would be enough for this quick trip to the market. Her perception of danger had been little more than a vague warning and she hadn't realized they were so close.

It was unfortunate that the clothing vendor, a friend of Nebet's, had called to her and asked how she liked Vidar while the two Hunters were close by. They'd each grabbed an arm and escorted her to a back alley. She couldn't allow them to take her back.

Before she'd escaped from her imprisonment, she'd decided that she would rather fight to the death than submit to being caught and returned. Those feelings hadn't changed. Fighting with all her strength to pull away from the two men, Ahnika kicked and screamed in the hope that someone would take the chance and help her. Or, if escaping her captors failed, she planned to make her retrieval so difficult they would just kill her.

As Raj moved close enough to intervene, he watched the men struggle to keep a hold on the twisting, snarling woman between them. She wasn't going with them willingly and her resistance kept Jondil and Zaben from noticing him. But Raj knew the men were very strong and she wouldn't get away on her own. Raising his arm to send a psychic blast toward the men, he stopped and cursed. Before he could release the bolt of energy, an angry Jondil knocked the woman unconscious with a stunning blow to the right side of her head. Raj watched in shocked disbelief as the men dropped her to the ground.

Raj's temper exploded. Thrusting a strong psychic punch to Jondil's head, he knocked him on his ass to sprawl in the dirt beside Ahnika. Following up with a quick exchange of solid energy blasts with Zaben, Raj stepped aside and Zaben's shot glanced off Raj's shoulder. Fortunately, one of

Raj's hits struck Zaben in the center of his chest, knocking the wind out of him. Raj's injury would hurt for a while but he was thankful it hit his shoulder and not his head, as he would have been knocked out and unable to help Ahnika in any way.

Jondil was out cold, and Zaben was on his knees unable to breathe. Running forward, Raj scooped Ahnika into his arms and immediately location-shifted with her. He moved in the direction of Tanar, resting after the first transfer long enough to make sure Ahnika was still breathing. Twice more, he gathered his strength and relocated. Pushing his abilities almost to the point of exhaustion, he moved them as far away from the other Hunters as he could manage.

Finally stopping beside a small lake, he felt they'd covered enough ground to allow them to rest and to give Ahnika time to regain consciousness. Concentrating on using his dwindling psychic reserves to shield them from anyone who tried to follow, he shook his head in private disgust. It seemed since he'd taken the job of looking for Ahnika, he hadn't had more than a *non* of time where he didn't have to worry when his next *Vampen* feeding was going to take place. *This is not the time or place for me to feed.*

Carefully laying Ahnika in the soft blue grass, he took off his robe. Checking to make sure she wore something other than her outer garment before gently sliding it from her body—he could well imagine her reaction if she woke after being terrorized to find herself naked with a man she didn't know. Glancing around the area, he scanned the small cove. They were nestled at the edge of a small lake of violet water. There weren't any places to hide or defend themselves in this pretty place, he would have to move quickly to wake her and get them somewhere more secure.

Before tending to his own injuries he would see what he could do for Ahnika. The side of her face was covered in dried blood so he quickly shrugged out of his shirt and ripped the sleeves out. Using one of the sleeves he'd torn from his shirt to dip in the lake, he then dropped to his knees beside her and gently cleaned the dirt and the small amount of blood from her face. The small cut had quit bleeding but she was still unconscious.

Raj moved his injured shoulder in a circle to try and release some of the tension, looking down he saw the wound was red and swollen but wouldn't require treatment. He absently used the wet cloth to clean the area, he had never been much of a healer so he wouldn't waste the energy trying to heal either his wounds or Ahnika's as they weren't life-threatening.

Leaning back against a small boulder while waiting for her to regain consciousness, he took the opportunity to study the woman he'd been seeking. Ahnika's tall, supple body was garbed in a modest emerald gown gathered lightly just under her breasts. The neckline made a slight vee and had a high collar, with long sleeves ending in points over the top of her hands. Only the unclaimed women of Zylar wore this dress design. It covered her completely from neck to ankle, but couldn't disguise her full curves.

Stroking a finger tenderly down the side of her face, he marveled at skin the color of a pale pinkish-red *Nui* fruit. Frowning in anger, he very carefully turned her head — at least the skin on one side of her face was pale red. The side where Jondil struck her was an angry purple.

Ahnika's eyebrows were a deep brown and arched perfectly over her closed eyes. She had full, pale pink lips, and her long brown hair, rich with red and blonde highlights was braided, it looked as if her hair would hang far past her waist. *Lovely*.

Raj restrained himself from taking more than a glimpse of her chest, only doing so to be assured she was still breathing regularly. His quick look told him she was amply endowed and he wondered for a *minon* if her nipples were the same pale pink coloring as her lips...

The red and blue aura surrounding Ahnika quivered, sending a tendril toward him. Groaning as one of the ribbons softly stroked his upper thigh—he slammed his mental shields in place. *She is hurt*, he mentally chastised himself, *I cannot be lusting after her like this. I just need to feed the Vampen hunger and this poor child is in no condition to help me. Remember that!*

Slowly moving his gaze back to her face, he found her studying him intently with soft, shimmering green eyes. Brac had been wrong when he told Raj her eyes were hazel. Very wrong.

Smiling reassuringly, he eased back a bit more and said, "Good, you are awake."

"Who are you? And where am I?" she demanded quietly.

"My name is Raj. Do you remember what happened to you in the market in Vidar?" he asked.

Frowning, Ahnika suddenly took a quick breath and tried to sit up, but Raj gently restrained her by placing one hand on her shoulder and holding her in place. "It's okay, you are safe."

"Those men who grabbed me—" she put her hand up to the side of her face, " —and hit me. Who were they? *Where* are they?" she cried.

"The men were Hunters sent by Brac to find you. I knocked them out for a bit, and then got you out of there. Using my ability to location-shift, I moved us several times so the men would have a difficult time finding us. However, I have no doubt that they or others like them are looking for us." Raj kept his voice calm and matter of fact. "Brac has many Hunters searching for you. I promise to help you escape them any way I can."

Ahnika scowled at him. "How do you know Brac is after me? Why would you do this for me? How am I supposed to believe you aren't one of them? Who are you?"

Raj laughed, careful to keep a *non*-threatening posture. "I will be happy to explain everything to you," he glanced around while he spoke. "But it's a rather long story and one better told when we are hidden and prepared to defend ourselves. I am shielding for now, but my psychic energy has almost been depleted because of the fight with your two would-be abductors and our escape this far. We need to find a cave or at least something solid to put at our backs while we rest so I only have to worry about keeping watch in one direction. Will you be okay while I scout around to find us someplace safe? Once we're settled, I'll explain everything to you."

At her nod, Raj stood to study the land around him and Ahnika took the opportunity to take a good, long look at her protector. Good Goddess, she recognized him! Before her stood the man from her dreams. The one she'd fantasized was her mate. Or...at least she *thought* he looked like the man. It had been so long since she'd allowed herself those dreams that she wasn't sure.

As he wore no shirt, her eyes caught and snagged on the smooth expanse of his chest, the deep golden skin and the rippling abs. Her eyes were drawn to the dark, deep rose circles of his nipples. Swallowing nervously, she moved her eyes only to become fixated on the slight trail of dark hair starting at his belly button and running down...she quickly yanked her eyes back to his face.

The man, who'd said his name was Raj, had very dark brown hair parted a little to the left side and falling well past his shoulders. His thick, dark eyebrows covered eyes such a pale, icy blue…the color was startling in its intensity. His face was roughly sculpted with high cheekbones and a broad, straight and almost regal-looking nose. A bottom lip slightly larger than the top, made his mouth look full and sensuous.

Licking her suddenly dry lips, she studied him warily, and wondered if she would be safe with him, if she could trust him with her story. The sudden physical attraction dulled her mind and she needed to be able to trust her senses.

Sighing in resignation, Ahnika realized she had little choice. Able to feel the menace and evil intent rolling off the two thugs in the market, she *didn't* believe Raj wanted to hurt her, or return her to Brac. Right now she felt…safe.

She wouldn't have had the strength to fight off the other men on her own, and she knew they hadn't given up as the sensation of evil coming closer rolled across her psychic aura in dark waves.

Watching as Raj searched for a safe place to rest, the violet lake caught her attention. Off to one side she noticed sheer cliffs tapering into the little cove where they'd stopped. She got the impression of… Ahnika stood and concentrated, her delicate features caught in a frown. Yes…she could detect a small waterway below the lake's surface leading into the cliff and a small cave.

Shuddering, she blocked unbidden memories from her mind.

There were thick stone walls that would protect them below, and it would be next to impossible for anyone to trace them through water and stone. But it would be like returning to her underground prison. She was unaware Raj had turned to study her as all of her attention was focused on the cave she'd located.

"What do you sense?" he asked quietly.

Ahnika turned to find Raj watching her intently. Would he believe her? "I am from the planet Zmar. We are a people who have adapted and who thrive in a watery environment. One of my...gifts, if you will...is the ability to trace underwater paths. Out in the water there is a passageway a few steps away from the land's edge, cutting back into the cliffs. At the end, there is a small cave that should shield us— or if we're discovered—will be an easier location to defend." She hesitated to see if he would accept her knowledge.

Raj believed her without question. After all, he had seen how she escaped from Brac's fortress. "I can't location-shift through stone walls with the little strength I have left. Can we swim this channel?" he asked.

He believed her! Smiling with relief, she replied, "Yes, it is not overly long."

"Then let's get moving. The other Hunters are getting closer by the *minon*." He silently thanked the Goddess that Ahnika trusted him, at least in this. He knew she was nervous about going into the water tunnel. It had to remind her of her escape from Brac's fortress. He could only imagine what she was going through. If they had any other choice— he wouldn't ask this of her.

Chapter Six

🙰

The narrow, submerged passage turned out to be longer than Raj calculated from Ahnika's swift description. The winding channel took them far into the side of the cliff, with enough pockets of air for them to easily negotiate its length. He believed they should be safe in this cave as he hadn't been able to sense its existence and he felt sure none of the other Hunters would have the talent to do so either.

Watching her closely as she walked out of the water and up into their haven, he grimaced as her breathing escalated and her eyes grew wide. When she started rubbing her hands up and down her forearms as if she were freezing, he set about making what changes he could.

A small cave, it was dry and had plenty of fresh air and muted light from Zylar's suns coming through several small fissures in the roof of the cave. Using the last of his psychic power, he called food, dry clothing and a soft pallet of blankets to their hideaway. For now, these few necessities would have to be enough. It was cold in the cave, but a fire was well beyond his energy level at the *minon* and he couldn't quite manage the steady output needed to fashion a light orb. Laying the blankets out on the ground, Raj motioned for Ahnika to rest between them.

Moving cautiously, Raj settled himself on the blankets beside her…close, but not touching. He did not want to frighten her or give her any reason to close herself off from him. Feeling a little overwhelmed, Raj could only blame his tension on the fact that he was tired. Physically and psychically tired.

As he sat beside her, Raj noticed Ahnika's muscles tensing, as if she were waiting for him to strike out at her in some way. Slowly he reached for some food, and settled back to give her time to relax. Guessing this situation would be hard for her, he moved only when necessary, wanting her to become comfortable with his presence.

He was so very aware of this woman, if her physical beauty or his inherent need to protect wasn't enough to generate an interest — then the added sensual assault of her pulsing aura created a sexual tension so strong it made him want to howl in stunned fascination.

Raj didn't think he would ever be calm or tension-free around her. Expending dwindling psychic energy to keep even the slight personal shielding in place was necessary to prevent her aura from sending him to his knees. By Zylar's moons, it was going to be a long night!

"Ahnika, would you like me to make you a cool compress to put on your cheek?"

She shook her head.

For several *minons* they were quiet, each intent on the food they were eating. After a while, Raj broke the silence. "I promised when we were safe I would explain everything — at least everything as I know it. The problem is, much of what I know is based on suspicions or an instinct the situation wasn't what it appeared. I am hoping you can clarify a few things for me as well," he said.

Ahnika looked at Raj, meeting his intense gaze. "Okay, I will try. Were you following me?"

Raj could see Ahnika holding her breath in anticipation of his answer. He decided to get it all out in a clean sweep.

"Yes. Brac hired me as a Hunter over a *setnon* ago." At Ahnika's terrified gasp and her attempt to jump up and flee, Raj gently secured her wrist in his hand and hurried to add, "But — and this is important, Ahnika — Brac didn't realize who he'd hired for the job. I track people in order to help those in need, not for the money. On Zylar, I am widely acknowledged as one of the best at what I do but it is also understood that I have very strong principles and am rather picky about those I work for. Brac didn't realize this. When I met with him, I didn't like Brac or the situation he painted for me. He hired me to find his missing daughter, but couldn't describe her or provide a holo-picture. And that, along with the psi-sensations I picked up from his residence, led me to believe there was more to the story than what he was telling me. Many other things didn't make sense, and all the conflicting pieces of information intrigued me enough to take the job, *despite Brac*. I decided to see what I could do to unravel the mystery of the missing daughter. You. If he *is* your father, I apologize for my assessment of him."

"I most definitely am *not* his daughter," Ahnika said vehemently.

"I never thought you were," he said smugly. "The telepathic ambiance coming from Brac's home was comprised of terror and an unwholesome malevolence. In my profession, it is imperative I trust my instincts. With my psychic evaluation at odds with his description, and the depressing atmosphere surrounding him, I became very skeptical of the entire situation. You said earlier you came from Zmar. How did you get to Zylar?" Moving with slow care, Raj released Ahnika's wrist and sat back as he tried to project a feeling of calm acceptance. He hoped she would pick up on his body language and really trust him with her secrets.

Can I do this?

She'd been on her own for so long and the only men she'd been alone with had hurt her. Somewhat reassured that her internal senses weren't screaming for her to run from Raj, she frowned when she considered her instincts were just the opposite. She felt like all she wanted to do was curl up in his arms and stay with him forever. Now *that* was crazy!

Ahnika looked closely at Raj and considered trusting him with her story. She closed her eyes for a *minon* to focus more clearly on her inner alarms instead of the compelling sight of the man before her. Nothing. There were no alarms, no sense of evil or the darkness she'd felt from Brac and the men he'd employed.

Did this mean her newly discovered abilities weren't effective because she was hidden away from the moons' rays, or did it indicate she could trust him with her story? Did she have a choice?

Over the last several *bi-nons*, Ahnika had come to the painful realization she'd never escape Zylar on her own and return to Zmar. Knowing she needed help from someone, she decided to take a chance on Raj. Maybe he really *was* the man she'd dreamed of, the man whose image she'd seen in her mind and in the water sculpture on Zmar. Maybe her dreams weren't to foretell the man as her mate, but because he was meant to be her defender.

When those thoughts brought a wave of comfort, she knew she'd guessed correctly. She would just ignore the accompanying disappointment. It was a shame that he couldn't be both.

She started speaking slowly, but, soon, the words of her story just seemed to tumble out of her. Beginning with her kidnapping from Zmar by men wearing the Zylan Ruler's crest, she then detailed her long confinement and the absolute atrociousness of Brac's activities. Without once looking at Raj, Ahnika finished with the story of her escape, and how she'd lived with Gardeil and Nebet in Vidar, which allowed her to research Zylar's ruling family and how she'd come to find out her captor was Brac. What she still didn't understand was what role the man played in Zylan society.

"I thought Gardeil could assist me in getting an introduction to the royal family…maybe with the Ruler's new Earth wife. I think I need to take the chance that Brac used the Ruler's crest without his knowledge and maybe Tar could stop Brac from hurting other women," she finished in a rush.

She could feel herself blushing, her already red skin growing flushed and hot as the increased blood flow made her cheek throb where the man had hit her. Pressing her palm to her bruised cheek, she tried to stop her tears from flowing. She couldn't believe she'd told him everything. Every sordid detail lay open and exposed and she waited silently for his condemnation. She was sure that he would find fault with her — he probably thought she took too long to escape. When he didn't immediately respond, her anxiety climbed with each breath of silence. When Raj jumped off the blanket and began to pace, she flinched in alarm. His silence and the dark emotion rolling from him in waves unnerved her. She pulled herself into a small ball in case he turned on her.

Raj didn't interrupt Ahnika's horrific tale, he listened first in disbelief and then in growing irritation and finally with absolute rage at the chronicle of what had been done to Ahnika. And, it had been happening for many life cycles and to many other women. When she got to the final piece and explained the false links and the sadistic training involved, he wanted to scream in fury.

He would kill Brac. Leaping to his feet, he struggled to bring himself under control. Ahnika drew back and seemed to shrink, refusing to meet his gaze. Seeing his rage, she believed he was mad at her when all he wanted to do was gather her in his arms and protect her from any further harm. Resisting the compulsion to drag her to him in a fierce need to comfort had to be the hardest thing he'd ever done…he was sure the action would frighten her.

"Raj?" Ahnika whispered sadly. "You don't believe me, do you? I *know* I should have tried to escape sooner but...I...I just couldn't..."

"Oh, Goddess, Ahnika, I believe you. And don't *ever* think you could have gotten away from him any earlier. I think you were extremely lucky to escape when you did. Look at me, sweetheart."

When Ahnika finally met his gaze, Raj knelt before her. "I am amazed at how well you have taken care of yourself thus far. Brac is a powerful man with many resources at his beck and call. I'm...just...I am so angry and sickened that anyone, especially a man who is a member of the Council of Ten, could do something so...so...well, words escape me. I wish I had been able to find you sooner."

Raj leaned forward and reached out to wipe a tear from Ahnika's cheek with the light brush of his fingers. "I wish...a lot of things had been different. But most of all, I do not want you afraid of me. The rage I feel inside is not for you and I promise I will do everything in my power to protect you and keep you safe from this *minon* on. My fury is directed toward Brac. To the things he has done and the lives he has ruined."

The sick feeling in his gut, regretting falling ill and being delayed from finding her when she'd first escaped, silenced Raj. When he was finally able to continue, he could see her react in shock to his words. "Damn, we have got to get out of here and get to Tanar. I am too psychically weak to contact my brother, Mica, by using mind-speak. Mica is Zylar's High Priest. And Zylar's Ruler, Tar, has been a friend to both of us since childhood. There is no question about their lack of involvement, Ahnika. When they hear your story, they will be as shocked and sickened as I am about the way Brac has been kidnapping and mistreating all of these women. In fact, knowing those two, I could almost feel sorry for Brac when they find out about what he has been doing."

Ahnika was elated with Raj's belief in her. Truly feeling she could trust his judgment when it came to the Ruler's involvement, she promised herself to rely on her instincts from now on. She was happy to turn the problem over to Raj, it was too large for her to solve on her own and something must be done soon for the other women left in Brac's prison. Looking at the earnest expression of pain and anger on Raj's face, she relaxed fully for the first time since her escape. Wondering at the attraction she felt for him, she debated if it could just be a by-product of her dreams. Or maybe she was drawn to him because of the feeling of safety generated in his presence. Whatever the reason—she focused on his every movement.

"We will have to walk for several *bi-nons* to reach the ruling city and I have a feeling the other Hunters will be on our trail the entire time."

Ahnika could tell that for some reason Raj was angry with himself.

"So we'll rest for now and start toward Tanar when your psychic energy has restored itself," she said.

Shaking his head, Raj laughed bitterly. "No, Ahnika. I'm afraid my psychic skills will be of little use to us. I am *Vampen*. Food and rest won't work to recharge my powers. I'll try to figure something out. I have never been strong enough to initiate mental communications with others but it's possible that Mica might contact me—his ability for mind-speak is strong enough to hold the conduit open between us. However, since he is newly mated, it could take *nons* for him to think of establishing such a link. But, for now, we are safe. We need to rest and allow your body to heal and for you to regain your strength. I promise nothing will happen to you while I'm here."

Ahnika wasn't ready to rest and she wanted to understand why he wouldn't be able to recuperate like most people did. She was also impatient to get to Tanar and get help for those other women. "I don't understand. What is *Vampen*? Why won't your abilities rejuvenate with rest?"

He sighed. This explanation would be difficult and he didn't want to alarm her so soon after she'd given him her trust. Carefully he searched his thoughts for the right words. "A *Vampen* is someone whose psychic powers aren't tied to the moons of Zylar. There have been only two of us born in the last thirty or so life cycles. My mother was kidnapped when she was pregnant with me and held for several *bi-nons*. She suffered the trauma of a mate's link separation during this time. Zmarians have the same mating links as the Zylans, correct? And you know linked mates experience extreme agitation and psychic pain if they are away from each other for very long?" he asked her.

Ahnika nodded her understanding and Raj continued, "The only other known *Vampen* is Tabor, a man of twenty life cycles whose mother's life was also endangered by a link separation during her pregnancy. My brother is a very skilled healer and he's been studying this for many life cycles. Consulting with the ancients and other healers throughout Zylar in his search for an answer to this puzzle, they have speculated that, somehow, this suffering our mothers went through breaks a normal bond to the moons. Tabor's powers differ from mine, but we share one trait—both of us need to feed psychically off another's energy to restore and to build our mental potency. Most Zylans regain their strength with exposure to Zylar's moons but this doesn't work for Tabor and me. We require something totally different."

When she remained quiet, as if absorbing what he'd said, Raj completed his tale. "There is more. Most Zylans have some sort of characteristic mark, which is used to foretell specific psychic abilities, but neither Tabor nor I have any such distinctive markings. Neither of us developed any paranormal powers until we'd reached full sexual maturity and attempted to reach orgasm with a woman. I have been found to have some…unusual…skills that the healers have never seen demonstrated by anyone else on Zylar. Not even Tabor. However, he could develop other abilities over the next several life cycles. No one is sure what to expect because there still isn't a lot known about *Vampens*."

Blushing at his mention of sex, Ahnika kept silent for only a *minon*. "So…if you fed off my energy, would you have enough vitality to get us to Tanar?" She refused to allow him to treat her as if she were fragile. If he needed to feed, he could do it from her so they could get where they wanted to be that much faster.

His body tightened and he clenched his fists in response to her innocent words as desire threatened to overwhelm his control. The entire time he'd been near her, Ahnika's aura kept trying to play along his skin. Having her offer to let him feed from her wonderfully lush body was enough to make him sweat. He shouldn't do it. It was a betrayal of her trust in him. But he wanted. Oh, Goddess, how he wanted this woman.

He started to say no to her when he remembered the surge of energy he'd received from the simple pleasure he'd experienced with her psychic trail. And, he still carried the vial of enhancement potion Shalan gave to him. If she took the potion, his heightened reaction to her soul trails might make it possible for him to feed enough to get them to Tanar. But in spite of her experiences with Brac, she was an innocent and it could harm her emotionally. He wouldn't — he couldn't — ask this of her. "It is not something I can ask of you little one, you have already been through too much."

"It would hurt me then?"

"No, it doesn't hurt, but…" he searched for the correct words, "in order for me to feed, your own psychic shields must drop. The only time our protective shielding disappears entirely is when we experience an orgasm. I cannot ask that of you, Ahnika. You've been through entirely too much, and I would be no better than Brac if I took advantage of you in this way. After all you've been through, I worry that the experience would be too much for you."

Now that almost made her mad. Who was he to say what was too much for her? This *fragile woman* thing was going too far. "After my experiences with Brac, I have a fear of being with any man. If I understand what you're saying, we would have sex and you would feed. I am not sure if I will be able to do this...but you have promised you wouldn't force me...or...hurt me. And I believe you," she stated quietly.

Raj frowned. "I would *never* harm you. And it doesn't need to be consummated sex—I don't have to enter you with my cock. All I need to do is to bring you to climax and I can guarantee you would find nothing but pleasure from the experience. But this is not something I'd want to put you through after your ordeal. You need time to heal from the ugliness of Brac's treatment and your first real experience with sex should be with your mate. Just go to sleep, Ahnika, I will figure out something else." His voice had grown rough, husky as he spoke of bringing her to climax—he could picture it all so clearly in his mind. It didn't matter how badly he wanted to bury his body deep within her softness, how talking about the situation increased his need to hear her cries of release...he would *not* succumb to his lusts.

"I'll sleep on it, Raj, but I want you to consider this. We have to remember our most important goal is to get us both to Tanar as quickly as possible so Brac can be stopped. To do this, you need your psychic powers or we're both at risk. I *know* you'll do every thing possible to keep me safe and protected but if anything happens to the two of us, no one will ever find out what Brac is doing and what atrocities he has committed. I don't want to take that chance, Raj. Yes, I've been through a horrible experience and I've seen and felt things no woman should ever be forced to endure. After all that has happened, I've lost most of my innocence and I'm sure my understanding of what takes place between a man and a woman is tainted but I truly believe you will not do anything to harm me. I would rather die than go back to that…place and I'm willing to do anything to stay out of Brac's hands so the other women can be freed quickly."

Raj started to speak, but she interrupted him. "I know I am not appealing to most men and that my body doesn't react as it should, but—"

This time he interrupted her. "How can you say that, Ahnika? You are a beautiful and desirable woman. It is normal for your body to react unfavorably to the pain and degradation Brac put you through. Sex and loving can be many things, but first and foremost, it must be consensual. Force or coercion will only serve to separate your mind from your body and both need to be engaged for you to achieve true pleasure. Any reaction you might have had during your captivity was right, and you will find your body's responses will be completely different when you choose to give yourself. If we decide to do this, you will always have control of the situation. At anytime you feel afraid, you need only to say the word…*stop*."

Looking at her sad eyes, Raj could almost see the conflicting emotions battling within her. How could she even think her body wouldn't delight him? Every breath she took brought his eyes to her chest and his body and mind struggled with conflicting urges, wanting to reach out and touch her velvet-soft skin, yet needing to reassure her of his trustworthiness—which would be blown all to Zylan hell if he fell on her like a rutting beast.

Eyes downcast she mumbled, "I was told…"

"You were told by whom? Brac? Or one of your other captors? I can only imagine the things they would say to you and those words would have no bearing on reality. Remember, they would say or do anything to hurt you, little heart. Do not even think their words would carry a kernel of the truth."

He stopped to gather his thoughts and realized he just couldn't discuss this yet. He had to think through the possible consequences if he were to feed from her. "We are physically and emotionally tired right now and I am having a difficult time processing all you have told me. I need to sleep. Let's wait and discuss this further tomorrow. There will be time after we rest to make any decisions and I need a clear head to consider all of the ramifications if I do or don't feed. Sleep, Nika, sleep and know you are safe with me," he said softly. The shortened version of her name fell from his lips and he intuitively knew it fit. *Nika.* How right it felt to call her this.

Nika. Smiling through her tears at the emotion in his voice, she couldn't believe Raj had inadvertently called her by her father's pet name, a name she hadn't shared with him. A strong feeling of warmth and safety seeped into her soul—something she hadn't felt since her capture. Only one thing would make her feel better.

"Raj. There is just one problem. This small place and the rock walls remind me too much of my cell. Will you hold me while we sleep? I don't want to wake up with nightmares, believing I'm back in my tiny chamber," she said in a small voice.

Groaning inwardly for what he knew was coming, he wanted to take her in his arms and comfort her but he knew—he just *knew*—it would be almost impossible to hide his body's reaction from her. If he held her, the red and blue vibration of her aura would drive him insane. But this comfort was not intended for his sake, this courageous and remarkable woman, who had lived through Zylan hell, needed him to simply hold her.

He rolled over on his side, and silently gathered her into his arms. Snuggling her back to his front, he let her use one of his arms as a pillow while he draped his other arm over her waist.

After a soft sigh, Ahnika settled quickly into sleep.

Nika trusted him. Raj felt as if he had been gifted with a unique and wonderful prize. Now he must honor that trust by keeping her safe, not only from the Hunters who followed them, but also from his growing desire for this woman.

It's only the Vampen need, he mentally chastised himself, *I can fight against it for her sake and offer only comfort.*

Shivet!

* * * * *

Raj woke first, and carefully moved his lower body back a few inches, away from the arousing nest it found cupped against Ahnika's slender form during sleep. His cock was so hard it felt as if it would burst at the slightest amount of pressure. Unsuccessfully, he tried to scan above their hiding place but his psychic resources were completely depleted. They'd only been asleep a short time, as the light in the cave attested to the suns still being visible in the sky.

Raj hadn't managed to come up with any alternatives to feeding his *Vampen* nature with Ahnika's passion. Not sure he'd even really tried, he was disgusted with himself with how even the thought of pleasuring her made his cock swell—to full and painful attention. Swearing silently, he kept reminding himself that he had more control than this.

Or maybe he didn't—the reaching tendrils of her aura kept him tense and on edge, he'd all but given up fighting against the teasing touch. Every time Ahnika so much as took a breath of air, the wisps would pulse and his cock would throb and expand. Because of his increasingly flimsy shields, the effect on him started to build and he burned.

In complete absorption, he watched as she rolled sensuously onto her back, her arm sliding out to find his thigh with her hand. Sucking in a harsh breath as his straining shaft jerked in hopeful eagerness, her eyelashes fluttered and lifted, her sleepy green gaze moved to find his.

"Hello," she said softly.

Raj gently withdrew his arm from under her head and propped his elbow up to allow him to look down on her. "Sleep well?" he asked quietly.

She smiled warmly as she glanced up and around and noticed the late afternoon sunlight. "Yes, very well. Are you feeling better after our short rest?"

Raj closed his eyes…his body had rested but his psyche hungered for what lay beside him. If she was still willing, he really had no choice. "Nika…"

"It's all right, Raj. Just tell me what you want me to do."

His body clamored at him to take her to peak fast and hard…but even with the potion, he would need multiple and intense orgasms from one woman to bring him to full power. And leaving their safe hideaway at anything less than full psychic ability could put Nika in danger from the other Hunters.

Raj needed the kind of orgasms that came after extended foreplay, hard and strung together for potency. But, more importantly, he wanted the experience to be special for Nika. Clenching his jaw, he took long, deep breaths as he struggled to bring himself under control. He longed to replace the ugliness of Brac with healing pleasure, but more than that, he wanted Nika's body beneath his. He couldn't think, couldn't decide if he wanted her to feed the *Vampen* within him, or if

he just wanted her for himself. This was not making sense —
he'd never felt anything like it before.

"I have a potion with me that was designed to increase
the energy a woman releases during orgasm. It requires you
to take just a drop and will not harm you. You will need to do
nothing but allow me to touch you. If you're still willing to
take this step, then I want you to promise me something. If at
any time you change your mind or something makes you
uncomfortable, you will tell me to stop. Promise me, little
one," he urged.

Ahnika nodded her head solemnly and sat up. Raj took
the vial of potion from its hidden pouch at his waist and
placed a small bead of the fluid on the tip of his middle
finger. He groaned silently as Nika's small pink tongue
slipped between her full lips to lap at the droplet. His penis
danced wildly when she then pulled the finger into her
mouth to suck him clean. Raj was stunned at his lack of
control, knowing he should be able to do better than this.

He managed to croak out, "We will go very slowly,
Nika. I want you to relax and enjoy this. I'll start with a light
massage that will help you to get comfortable with my touch.
Please take off your dress and lay facedown on the blankets."

Hesitating, Nika knew her back was a network of small
scars, testament to the beatings she had endured from her
captors. She could only imagine what the damage would look
like and she was afraid to give him another reason to think
her ugly. "My back isn't a pretty sight, Raj," she stated sadly.
"I do not think you should start there."

Raj frowned at her and, standing, he held out his hand to
Ahnika. She took the offered help and he pulled her gently to
her feet. Placing his hands on her shoulders, he allowed them
to slowly smooth down her back to her waist where he
paused. With infinite patience, he caught the back of the
dress and began to lift it upwards. When the hem of her

gown reached her waist, he gathered the fabric in his hands and raised it over her head in one tender movement, and then tossed it to one side.

Ahnika wore no undergarments. Stepping back two short, small steps so he could see her better, Raj gazed in silent awe at the vision before him.

She was breathtaking. The exceptional beauty of her light red skin was a temptation too strong to ignore, he reached out his hand to lightly run his fingers over her shoulder...she was so soft. A deeper blush of red bloomed across her face and upper chest, covering her generous breasts. Breasts crested with full, deep burgundy areolas and darker puckered nipples.

Raising his gaze, Raj caught the look of uncertainty in her bright green eyes. "You are so lovely," he said hoarsely. Wanting to explore every inch of her, he glanced down to see tight auburn and gold curls at her woman's nest. *Later.* Telling himself he couldn't just fall on her in a mad fervor didn't seem to help a whole lot. Breathing deeply, he allowed the spicy fragrance of her growing arousal to envelop him. *This was not helping.*

With trembling hands, Raj turned Ahnika until her back was to him, and using his fingers, he worked her hair from her braid, finger-combing her long tresses as he let his shields drop and invited her colorful life force to tease along his nerve endings. Not wanting to fight the soul tendrils' effect on his body, he was afraid doing so would somehow restrict the flow of needed psychic energy. Raj still wasn't prepared when their touch caused his desire for this woman to grow beyond endurance.

Her glorious hair fell over his hands in soft waves to the back of her knees. Reaching up, he massaged her scalp and pulled her against his front. Bending to whisper in her ear, "I will love having your hair spread over my body, teasing me with its silken luxury. You take my breath away, Nika. Lie down for me on your stomach. Let me worship your beautiful body the way it is meant to be worshipped."

Raj helped her to first kneel and then to lie facedown on the blankets. He gathered her hair in his hands and helped to arrange it so that it fell to one side, out of the way for the massage she was about to receive.

Ahnika could barely breathe. Her eyes teamed with unshed tears. For the first time in so many life cycles, she felt beautiful. Felt cherished. She didn't feel as if her marred skin would disgust Raj. Her body and soul warmed to his touch, the sizzling awareness of the strong, gentle man at her back brought her an enthusiasm for more. There would be no question of calling a halt to this experience.

With the hair out of the way, her back was exposed to his sight. He drew in his breath. A collection of fine white lines crisscrossed her back and he could only imagine what they would look like in bright light. He shuddered as he visualized her delicate skin being punished and the pain she would have felt, moaned when the ghost echoes of her agony raked across his flesh. He would definitely kill Brac for this alone.

"Oh, little one, I wish I had been able to spare you this pain," he murmured as he bent over her back. Gently he moved his mouth and tongue over her skin, tracing each and every line, ministering to every past hurt.

Taking his time, he worshiped every inch of her exposed flesh starting at her neck, and working his way down to her feet. While he used his tongue and hands on her body, the red and blue tendrils of her soul reached out to stroke him, mimicking his movements and driving him to heights of tortured sexual arousal he'd never before experienced.

Chapter Seven

∽

Ahnika's pulse skipped a beat with the first touch of his mouth at the nape of her neck. Then it thundered in her veins as he suckled and lapped, nipped and stroked every inch of her backside. Each gentle, moist stroke seemed to ignite every inch of flesh he touched and sent darting spikes of heat to her core.

Her body reacted, swelling with a throbbing ache starting in her breasts and vibrating through her center. Her woman's channel felt engorged and wet and her body hummed with anticipation. Gasping aloud at the feel of his hands skimming along her sides as he stroked his fingers over the swollen edge of her breasts, she shifted and used her arms to push her body up enough to allow those hands to slide under her, to give his fingers room to torment her nipples. The combined sensations of his tongue teasing along her spine and his fingers plucking lightly on the taut points made her moan in delight.

Carefully, Raj rolled Ahnika onto her back. Stretching out beside her, he moved his upper body over her to capture her mouth in a kiss. Her inexperience showed, her lips were closed to him so he feathered his tongue lightly along the seam and flicked his thumb across her nipple. At her gasp of delight, he dipped into the honeyed splendor of her mouth. Drinking in her moans, he gloried in her body's uninhibited response and moved between her legs without breaking the kiss to nudge her thighs apart, settling his covered erection against her heat.

Using his tongue to glide in and out of her mouth in a slow parody of mating, he pushed his hips forward to rock slowly against her clit, driving her passion higher. His body railed at him. Never had his cock burned and ached like this, his nipples felt as if they were on fire and he slowly moved his hand down her arm and wrapped his fingers around her wrist to bring her palm up to brush against his chest.

His skin was bathed in the swirling and stimulating essence of her soul until every inch of his flesh pulsed with need. He was unable to contain a groan of pleasure at her tentative explorations. He loved the feel of her hands on his body, her fingers as they traced and molded the contours of his shoulders and back.

Panting, Nika tore her mouth from Raj. The impressions spiraling through her were unbelievable. She had such a clear awareness in her mind of what Raj felt, she could sense him...feel the tightness and sensitivity of his flesh as his body burned for her. It was almost as though their bodies were merging — the entwining passion seemed to grow and pound within her.

She had never imagined that being with a man could feel this good — she only knew she never wanted it to end. And, she desired — no, *wanted* — more. "You're still dressed," she complained breathlessly. She wanted his pants gone and she really wanted the hard ridge that had been tormenting her through the layers of his clothing buried deep within. The added ecstasy of sharp and rhythmic internal pinching within her nipples and between her thighs escalated her hunger. Nika's entire body burned with the intensity of her craving.

"Goddess, Raj, don't make me wait any longer I can't take it. Ohhhh."

"Oh, sweetling, there is so much more I want to do with you and if I take my pants off, it will be over for you too quickly. I want to savor you." Raj was having his own problems concentrating. Nika's hands slid up and down his chest, raking back and forth over his nipples as he had shown her. Each pass of her sweet flesh caused a chain reaction within him. A tight, sharp vibration shot from his nipples to his groin and caused his cock to twitch and expand with impatience.

Feeling as though the ripe head of his shaft would burst from each roll of exquisite sensation—he was confused. As a *Vampen*, his ability to be in command of his lust was legendary. This loss of control stunned him. His reactions had to stem from a side effect of her soul tendrils and his urgent need to feed. Not from his body's response to her soft hands raking over his skin and the feel of her cradled beneath him.

No. Raj chastised himself. There could be nothing different about this feeding. It was all about his requirement for psychic power and her need to survive. All she could be to him was a willing body to slake his *Vampen* hunger, a means to an end.

Shaking his head in disgust at his inner turmoil, he pressed his shaft against the sensitive flesh between her thighs and lowered his mouth to slowly suck one of her nipples between his teeth. Suckling her, he played for long *minons* with the tight bud, lightly biting. Breathing deep, he savored the unique and wonderful scent that was Ahnika, her fragrance reminded him of sunshine and the slightly tangy salt smell of the ocean.

Her breasts were magnificent, soft and plush and more than he could fit in one handful. Glorious burgundy nipples surrounded by the tempting satin circles of a subtly lighter color were large and puckered into hard nubs, which grew longer and harder the more he paid attention to them. It seemed as though she had been made strictly for his pleasure. His mouth covered first one breast and then the other as he divided his attention between them.

Moaning and frantically clutching his head, she arched into his delicate touch as he teased and tasted her, rolling her pert nipple against the roof of his mouth and then releasing it to torment the other. Her escalating cries of passion filled the cave as she screamed his name over and over. Begging him to take her.

Slowly, he kissed his way down her body, taking the time to ravish each inch of her skin, sipping first at her belly button and moving on to lave the lush arch of her lower stomach. The soft curls hiding her sweet-scented mound were moist with yearning and he drew more of her body's stimulated perfume into his lungs. Arousal blasted through him, causing a sharp ache in his chest and the burning need to mate with her increased.

No. Not mate, I can't mate with anyone until I find my Life Companion. It was only the need to feed from her that increased.

"Open for me," his voice hoarse as he commanded her, "I want to see you."

Timidly she did as he demanded and moved her legs wider. He put his hands between her thighs and parted her labia. Rumbling started deep in his throat at the vision of the rosy, swollen tissue of her labia. Weeping for him, her sweet cream oozed from her tight passage. Lifting her hips so he could position her for his mouth, he buried his face between her legs — intent on capturing her essence on his tongue.

Squealing in astonishment, she whimpered and tried to shut her thighs at the first slow swipe of his tongue over her clit. Raj used his elbows to keep her open to him, refusing to allow her to escape this pleasure. Closing his eyes, he lost himself in the taste and feel of this incredible woman. Ignoring the pull of her fingers in his hair, he worshipped her rich flesh with his mouth. Flickering and stabbing against her, then plunging his tongue into her liquefied core, he forced her now uninhibited response higher.

He smothered attention upon her hardened bud, dragging his tongue over her again and again until her hands held him in place instead of trying to push him away. Sobbing and thrusting her hips to meet him, she finally succumbed to his fevered caress.

With every previous *Vampen* feeding in his life, Raj had felt the power sizzle and grow around him. But Shalan's potion seemed to work especially well on Ahnika — the energy pouring from her to him seemed to build in magnitude far surpassing anything he'd felt before. With the roll of potent force came a separate craving, the longing to please and claim this woman, as he'd never wanted another. Not just to feed, but to share her passion. The thought flitted through his mind and he groaned, humming his discontent against her flesh. *If only.* He tried to convince himself it was just the added experience of the ever-present soul trails. Those tendrils were an integral element of her sensual nature. He loved having both her body and her psychic essence combined in such an erotic way.

"I can't, oh Goddess, it's too much, Raj. Ohpleaseohpleaseoh!"

Smiling at her wanton pleas, he kept his mouth over her and carefully pushed a single finger into her tight sheath. As he expected, he found the thin membrane and used his fingernail to carefully break it as he used his tongue to vibrate her to peak in an attempt to distract her from the pain. So consumed by Ahnika's taste, by his own needs, he totally forgot his plan to keep her a virgin.

Ahnika came with a wild scream. Arching her back in sensual agony, her hips left the pallet in an untamed shift that threatened to remove him. Lightly holding her hips, he followed her movement and continued his sensual assault until she begged him to stop. Energy poured into him from her long, rolling climax. Her shields dropped and the waves of heat and desire crashed through him, tugged at him with a brilliant flash of color and madness. In his delight at her response, he ignored the sharp, pinching pain in his nipples.

Desire burned hot and heavy in his bloodstream and he felt he would explode if he didn't take her now. Rising to his knees, he used a small bit of the psychic energy she released within him to rid himself of his pants.

Raising himself over Ahnika, he positioned the pulsating head of his cock in front of her wet slit. The knifelike stab of pleasure roaring through his body was a new experience for him. It seemed as if the red and blue whispers of sensation emanating from her soul twisted, turned, enveloping him a firestorm of passion beyond his control. The swirling vortex seemed to draw him down, connecting him to Ahnika.

In a heated rush, he lost all mental command over his body. Bending to take her lips in a hot, wet kiss, he used his lips, teeth and tongue and fed as if starving from the tangy sweetness of her mouth. Wild for him, Nika arched her sweet cunt up against him, trying to force him to slip into her passage. The *minon* his cock entered the moist and swollen passage into her body, everything descended into chaos.

A starburst of power exploded behind their eyes and energy slammed through Ahnika and into Raj like a blast of heat lightning. Shocking red and blue bolts of power drove into him and exploded in every cell of his body. Bellowing in mingled astonishment, pain and pleasure, he convulsed in reaction trying to cradle her beneath him as if he could protect her from the onslaught of untamed force.

In a vibrant backlash, the power rolled out of him and slammed back into her, quickly returning to him in a spiraling burst of energy that his greedy cock acknowledged with a powerful surge of length and thickness. Completely shaken, his mind was far beyond comprehending the fact he had found his mate and had somehow failed to recognize her from the beginning. Any thought of making sense of this failing was quickly driven out of his brain with his body's demand for complete attention.

He felt his Companion Links boiling up through his skin, emerging from the end of his cock with an unbearable burst of pleasure-pain. The sharp wrench of mating links breaching the tips of his nipples caused him to flex his hips and he thrust to the hilt, his balls slapping against her buttocks.

Ahnika yelled long and loud. She could feel the erotic bite of pain at both her breasts and between her thighs, as a fierce reaction seemed torn from her soul. The burning sensation and sharp desire coursing through her body signaled her links rising within her. The Companion Links shifted beneath her skin as the first of the delicate gold chains broke through the flesh at her nipples and clit.

The sharp pain of the links initiation screamed throughout her aching body and was immediately replaced with pleasure and a soothing merge of spirits between her and Raj. Unable to grasp a coherent thought except one... *I was right!* The man in her dreams so long ago was indeed her Life Companion. Her link mate.

Struggling to pull in enough air to supply her lungs, her breath left her on a gasp as her flesh started to throb where the links left her body. Strung tight, she pulsated with the need for more—more of *what* she had no idea, as his cock still filled her completely.

"Mine!" Raj growled. "Minemineminemineminemine."

"Yessss," Ahnika hissed. "Oh, Goddess! Yes."

Raj's entire being was obsessed with claiming the woman he had discovered as his Life Companion. Blind with overwhelming emotion and the physical need for his mate, he surged forward with the all-consuming urge to conquer and possess. *His.* Bound to him for their life spans, she would always be at his side or close enough to call—he finally felt complete.

Her internal muscles pulsed around him, gripping the thick flesh of his cock. She had been made for him. Only for him. Bracing his hands on either side of her head, he demanded, "Look at me, my mate. Keep your eyes on mine as we join our bodies and our lives together."

Ahnika whimpered and complied. The eyes she lifted to meet his were glazed with passion and need. The need for what only he could give her.

He started to move within her, slowly at first, and then increasing the cadence until he was slamming against her softness. Their bodies made wet, slapping sounds as they strove to become one. Initiating the links' vibration for the first time, he added a humming sensation to her breasts and pussy while he pummeled into her soft channel. The joining and use of the links proved to be too much, sending her immediately to a hard peak. With a strangled cry, she exploded around him as he convulsed over her with an echoing bellow of pure satisfaction.

Opening the links created a tie allowing them to share in each other's pleasure. They merged into a single consciousness, feeling their own orgasm as well as each other's. Acting as a conduit for his hunger and her yearning, the fused connection of their links caused their bodies to pulse with the tempo set by his shaft. The sensations spiraled between them, building, returning, crashing through the two of them, and exploding in a burst of light.

* * * * *

Raj lay stunned. The shock of discovering Ahnika was his Life Companion combined with the amount of power that poured into him and from their mutual climax overwhelmed him. Knowing only his link mate would be able to take his climax and convert both her peak and his to the psychic energy a *Vampen* required, he'd never have believed how amplified the psychic strength would be.

Looking at his sleeping mate, he lovingly used his power to cover their bodies with warm blankets. Since he now had energy to spare—and he would never again need to worry about his next feeding—he used a simple thought to simultaneously light a fire and convert the small cave into a sumptuous nest. Between one blink of an eye and the next, colorful carpets covered the floor and silk drapes hid the stone walls and glowing stones were set into the ceiling. Zylar's moons were out in the night sky, but their radiance did not extend to the chamber. He didn't want Ahnika to wake in the dark in a stone chamber. If he could do anything to prevent it, he wanted nothing here to remind Nika of the time she'd spent in Brac's prison.

Torn between the need to take care of Brac and his atrocities immediately and the knowledge that it would have to wait, he understood they wouldn't be going anywhere. As a newly linked couple, he and Nika would have to remain in their hideout for three *bi-nons*. The insatiable mating fever created between new Life Companions would keep them locked together in passion and make travel impossible. Even in sleep, the subtle vibrations of the links would keep them constantly aroused during this time.

Already he hungered for her. Careful not to awaken her, he bent over and used his minimal healing skills to reduce the bruising left by Jondil and to remove any residual soreness from their mating. She had been a virgin and he had not used her body gently. Raj would have her feeling only pleasure from their joining, not pain. Never pain. In a *minon* he would wake her with a kiss but first, he would contact his brother and warn him about Brac.

Mica, can you hear me?

Raj? Where are you? Where have you been? What happened, little brother? You are much stronger along our mental path. I have no need to force the connection.

I have found my Life Companion, Mica! One of the benefits to our mating appears to be a magnification of my powers.

Raj, this is wonderful! Who is she? Where? How did you find her? Ahhh. It's the woman you've been seeking.

Yes. It's a long explanation and one I have no time to go into right now. Already the fever is making this conversation difficult. Ahnika and I will be in Tanar in four bi-nons. *With my expanded powers, we should be able to travel quickly when the mating fever has diminished. I only want to warn you —*

Wonderful, I will tell the others and arrange a mating ceremony for —

No. That is not what I need to warn you about. The ceremony will to have to wait. I'm contacting you to tell you Brac is doing evil things, Mica. Very evil things. I don't want to go into detail about what I have learned without Ahnika adding her story. There are many reasons she needs to be completely involved with bringing him to justice. You will not believe what he has done. I know you were going to look into his dealings as I had such a bad feeling about the man. Don't do it, Mica. Don't alert him to any suspicion. He is dangerous and may strike at Nyssa or Tala...or Tar, for that matter. Please be careful and wait for us to explain what he is up to.

Ahnika stirred and pressed her back against Raj's chest as she woke. He had obviously gathered her into his arms after she'd fallen asleep. The advantage to this position occurred to her as she rubbed her body against him and felt his hard shaft pressed against her ass. Pulling the hand resting on her waist up to cover her breast, she rocked her hips back against the warm heat of his cock and she burned with a fierce need for her mate.

Raj gasped. As he was linked to Mica, the sound and a projection of what he felt spilled through their psychic link.

Raj. Break the link! I got your message and will stay away from Brac. Get back to your mate but sever the link. There is only so much brothers need to share!

Mica's laughter rumbled in his head as Raj closed the link between them and turned his undivided attention to his mate. Her body was restless, hungry for his touch. Anticipating the pleasure they would share over their mating time and the things he would teach her both now and in the many life cycles to come, he kissed the back of her neck with tenderness.

Moving his hand at her breast, he used his fingers to trace the delicate link chains hanging from her nipples. Flicking a finger over the tip, the swaying metal strand could be used to stimulate and tease. Enjoying the feel of her in his hands, he opened the links' path between them and used their mystical connection to create the feel of tongues lapping every one of her erogenous zones. While he lapped and laved her ear, plunging and retreating into its small recess, the link-created tongues stroked the bend of her elbow, behind her knee and one metaphysical mouth laved the sensitive spot at the nape of her neck, and another teased along the indentation of her hip.

Ahnika gasped, her body thrown into the fire of the links' appetites and Raj's touch, every nerve ending and sweep of flesh was teased into screaming arousal. No thought but to let Raj mold her body as he would, her only desire was to keep the incredible sensations flowing over her.

He lifted her leg up and settled it over his thigh, spreading her open so he could position his shaft to rub along her slit, she moved with him, encouraging...demanding. He chuckled in her ear and she felt the added link sensation of suckling mouths at her breasts. Biting, laving and pulling at her turgid nipples, the mouths joined their efforts to the symphony of pleasure Raj played over her body. Keeping each touch constant, never taking anything away, he added a new torment to her over-stimulated senses.

"Oh, Goddess. Raj!" she screamed. When pulsing vibrations started within her pussy, he pushed her to madness, with the teasing presence of his cock slipping into her vagina an inch, then out, breaching her again. In. Out. The excruciatingly slow tempo made her scream in frustration. She would kill him if he didn't—

"Fuckmefuckmefuckmefuckme," she shouted. Words she didn't think she'd ever say were pouring from her, explicit in their demand.

With a primal growl, Raj flipped her onto her stomach and maneuvered her into a crouch with her head down and the rounded globes of her sweet ass sticking up in the air. He moved to bind her long hair to one side, delighting in the sight of it spilling across her back and hissing when it whispered over his groin as he rearranged it. Pausing to relish the sight, until Nika started to complain, he thrust forward and impaled her with his thick cock, filling her to overflowing.

Her triumphant scream reverberated in the small space, "*Yes!*"

His control snapped as soon as her tight muscles clenched around his shaft and started to milk him. Her aura surrounded him as the tiny tendrils reached out to stroke along his flesh and consume him with fire and heat. Experimenting, he allowed the whispers of her soul to touch him and then tried to direct his aura to toward Nika. The resounding spike of sensual heat seared his skin and her panting shrieks assured him she felt the sensations as well.

Too much. Surging hot and hard, he hammered into her, holding her hips firm against him so he could piston and slam to his heart's content. To his cock's content. The appendage seemed to have taken on a life of its own, growing and expanding within her suctioning heat until he felt as if his head would explode. He kept the sensual thrill of psychic mouths and tongues playing over her body and opened the links to share in the absolute ecstasy he found buried deep within her. The shared passion coiled between them, intensifying each time it ricocheted from one to the other.

Mating links allowed them to feel each other's pleasure when they were open. Raj felt what she felt and her mind subtly directed his movements as she shared her need so he knew how to stroke, how deep to plunge. Through their link, he shared his body's reaction to the sensation of her hot sheath closing around him, the burning prickle of need radiating from the base of his spine, making his balls tighten in preparation, he slammed once more into her depths and felt her body and her response as if it were his own.

"Ican'ttakeit!" Her mind shut down, unable to deal with the interchange of orgasmic pleasure beating through her body and soul as their self-awareness united and intermingled. Hers to his and back again, the vibrations spiraled higher filling her heart, her soul, her body with his presence.

Keening noises and guttural yells escalated in volume as the explosion rocketed between them and proved to be too much. As power and energy burst—fusing their souls together, their minds tumbled into unconsciousness. For a short time, the linking fever was satiated.

Chapter Eight

ဆ

"Oh, dear Goddess, I am starving!" Still half-asleep Ahnika grumbled.

Raj laughed and swatted her beautiful ass. "As you should be, my love. If you would open your eyes, you would see a feast waiting for you to rejoin the living!"

She huffed and sat up, pushing her wild hair to one side and opening her eyes to the magical transference of their small cave. It looked like the inside of one of the richest homes with yellow, red and blue silk walls replacing the stone surface, and plush carpets on the floor. Lunar globes cast a golden glow from the ceiling and yes—thank the moons—there was food. Every delicacy and treat known had been piled before her. Closing her gaping mouth, she couldn't resist teasing him. "You've been busy. I take it psychic power or the lack thereof—is no longer an issue."

Reaching out, she plucked a delicacy from the tray and nibbled while she looked around in amazement.

He snorted. "Sweetheart, the power created between the two of us could handle the needs of the entire planet. Just tell me if I've missed something and I'll be happy to create it for you," he said smugly.

Swallowing her food, she replied without hesitation, "A bathing pool...with *hot* water." She knew she could bathe in the lake...but it was cold and if he could— "Oh!" And, just that quickly, one appeared in the corner. A beautiful rock pond, with a small waterfall cascading into the pool, had been added to the cave. Steam rising from the water's surface attested to its heat. The sound of water falling into the grotto with soothing whispers—an indication of its designer's creativity. "Dear Goddess, now I don't know if I should eat or bathe first."

Raj smiled indulgently. "Do both. Go get in the water and I will bring a plate of food and join you. I think we need to use this little break to talk and to rest—at least for the short time the links will allow us."

At the reminder of their mating, Ahnika suddenly felt a slight blush of embarrassment at her nakedness. Hurrying over to the pool, she slipped into the water and was unable to suppress the groan of pleasure as the warm liquid embraced her. Drifting for a *minon* in time, she kept her mind a careful blank. Taking this simple pleasure, she would block out all the things she didn't want to examine too closely. *Like being mated.*

Not blocking hard enough.

Raj's cock sat up and danced a jig at her small moan. *Short break.* When he glanced at Ahnika's face and read the confusion and panic in her eyes, he noticed how the links started vibrating with her bewilderment. Praying to the Goddess for just a little control, he needed to spend some time taking care of and talking with his mate. She needed to be courted and soothed into accepting their linking, not just with her body...but with her mind.

The moons knew this had been a shock to him...she must be reeling with the turn her life had taken. Willing his body into submission, he walked over to the pool with the tray of food strategically placed to prevent her noticing his rampaging cock. If he could have managed it without drawing attention to the state of his arousal, he would have thrown himself into the cold water of the lake.

Instead, he slid into the caress of warm water and kept a considerable distance from his bride, setting the tray of food on a nearby rock.

Ahnika sat up, careful to keep her body submerged in the lilac water as she glanced cautiously at Raj and smiled sheepishly. "Not exactly the results we were expecting." He could feel her resolve to not run from her fears.

Laughing full heartedly, Raj agreed, "No, little minx, I would have to say I was completely surprised by the result of our *Vampen* feeding." Handing her some of the fruit from the plate, he watched her eat and hesitated for a *minon* before saying, "Talk to me, Nika… Tell me how you are feeling."

Shrugging her shoulders she sighed. "I don't know. My feelings are all jumbled up inside of me. I'm amazed Shocked. Happy. Frightened. Confused. They seem to be in a chaotic tumble, each one taking hold only to be pushed aside by a new emotion. I had no idea the sexual pleasure could be so…"

"Cataclysmic…breathtaking…mind-blowing…stupendous…"

Her giggle eased his heart. "Yeah, that! But I keep thinking it all happened so fast. We don't *know* each other. We stumbled into this so how can it be right? How can you love…?" She stopped. Raj could feel her embarrassment at having voiced the concern.

"How can we love each other?" he said softly.

Ahnika hung her head unable to look at him.

"Sweetheart, look at me." When she met his gaze, he continued. "You know there is only one link mate for each person. Many people go their entire lives without making that ultimate connection. Our Ruler, Tar, couldn't find his mate here on Zylar. Mica searched multiple dimensions and several worlds for her, and it took him many life cycles to find Nyssa for Tar. When he found her, because she wasn't Zylan he had to create companion links for her body." Ooops. *Shivet*, he probably should have left that part out.

Nika gasped and started to sputter. He could feel her anger start to grow and focus, but before she managed to get her mind around the implication of what he'd said, Raj quickly continued.

"Mica used tendrils from both Tar's and Nyssa's souls to fashion *true* links, Nika. They were not the perverted version Brac came up with. Only Nyssa's body would accept the unique bonds created for her. They work the same way ours work, without using a box to generate pain, and they look the same. If you didn't know she wasn't Zylan-born, you wouldn't be able to tell."

Looking very unsure, she finally nodded her acceptance. Something about his explanation of links teased the back of her mind.

"The point I am so terrible at making, my pet, is that Tar and Nyssa love each other. Now. When she first came from Earth, she had a very hard time adjusting to our planet, to our ways. Nyssa said that even the sky and the water in her world are different colors than on Zylar. And Earth only has one sun and one moon. She wasn't used to the way women are treated here, and she is working to change that. But with such an extreme alteration of her life, she still grew to love Tar. I have no doubt that, in time, you will grow to love me as well. As I already love you," he said softly.

Ahnika closed her eyes and moaned silently. Tears seeped from under her eyelashes and rolled slowly down her face. "Oh, Raj. I wasn't worried about me being able to love you... I think the *minon* I opened my eyes and found you bending over me, washing my face...the seeds of love were sown. Your soul cries to mine and I know you are my true mate." She glided through the water and into his arms, her long hair floating behind her.

The links pulsed through them with impatient need.

For several *minons* he just held her. The Goddess had truly blessed them when they found each other. Bringing his hand to her chin, he raised her green-eyed gaze to meet the heat in his blue stare.

"I will love and cherish you for all time, Nika," he said reverently. Deliberately. Slowly. He reached out and cupped her face. Drawing his finger down her cheek to the side of her mouth and slid his thumb over her soft, pale pink lower lip and stroked a small caress there, fascinated by its promise. Remembering the taste of her—unforgettable, sweet. Addicting.

Heat flared between them. Smoldered. Ahnika inhaled sharply, "Raj." There was an ache in her voice.

His fingers curved around the nape of her neck, sifting through the cool wet tendrils of her hair. Nothing mattered to him but touching her, tasting her. His entire focus centered on getting close to her, skin against skin, as he anticipated the *minon* when he would bury his body deep inside hers. The links between them channeled an inbred need to claim her again, to remind her that she was his and his alone.

She could feel the desire through the links, swamping them both. Could feel his body hurt, needing to be joined to hers. He leaned down just as she strained upward to find his mouth with hers.

He kissed her then, a long slow kiss that built into a spiraling curl of heat, using every fiber of his being to blend hot passion, building love and possession. Mouths clinging together, their slippery bodies moved from side to side, rubbing...deepening the fire between them.

Wrapping her arms around his neck she pressed her body closer to his, her tongue slid along his teeth, teasing his tongue and drugging his senses with her intoxicating response. His fist bunched in her hair and his mouth fused with hers as he held her to him.

His mouth plundered hers as he explored the tender flesh between her lips, and used the links to fill her mind with his love. There was instant, urgent need as a tidal wave of heat poured over both of them. The links vibrated, sending their desire higher.

Feeling her wet breasts press against his chest as she wrapped one leg around his thigh, her steamy core pressed invitingly against his cock. Growing need spiraled out of control. He swept one hand over her side until he found her breast and began to play with the smooth nipple, teasing the pale burgundy nub of flesh until it hardened under his touch. When she started to keen and gyrate against him, he switched to her other breast to repeat his actions and then moved to trace the contours of her hip and to open his palm over her buttocks.

Catching her other leg, he guided it around his waist and lifted her into position over his straining shaft. The link fever built fast, pushing him to join his body to hers. Their shared consciousness, a persuasive ingredient in the urge to race to completion, made taking their time out of the question. Promising himself to luxuriate in a slow seduction sometime soon, he bent to the links' call for their joining.

He aligned their bodies, holding onto her hips with both hands to stroke his wet tip across her slick folds. He teased her, allowing only the ripe head of his penis to dip into her tight sheath. Ahnika's mewling sounds drove him crazy. Opening her link to him, so she could feel what he felt and burn while he burned, he held her immobile while he pressed firmly inside. Savoring the sensation of her tight sheath relaxing enough to allow him entrance, he threw back his head as the breath left his lungs in a sudden rush and the now familiar pulsation of the links stoked the fire between them.

Using those links, he caused them to thrum with power as he began pushing his hunger and her yearning back and forth with the tempo set by his shaft. A shudder of startled pleasure unbalanced her and she braced her hands on his shoulders.

"Do you like that, Nika?" he purred in her ear.

"Goddess, *yes*."

So tight and hot, she gripped him with a fierce keening appetite every bit as urgent as his own. Pushing against him, riding his body with an answering madness as he thrust up and into her. She used her thighs to squeeze his waist, her arms around his neck to lift off him, only to slam back. Keeping his hands on her hips, he helped her movements and lost awareness of everything but the joy of burying himself deeper and harder with each stroke.

Ahnika thought of nothing but the pleasure, and Raj. She could feel the heaviness in her body that signaled her climb toward release, too soon becoming a flash of fire between them that ignited hard and instantly sent them freefalling. Their bodies slapped together and churned the water around them, the water splashing back against them adding to the overload of tactile sensation.

Clinging to him, she dug her fingers into the hard muscle of his shoulder, attempting to take back some control and ride slower, wanting to curb the gathering force. It was too late. Her body rocked and rippled as they came together in a burst of heat. The links channeling an ever-growing progression of explosive ecstasy between them and their cries rang out together.

Raj held her in his arms until their heartbeats calmed. Carrying a sleeping Nika out of the water, he dried them both with a thought and took her to bed. They could eat later.

Three *bi-nons* had passed when they prepared to leave the cave. Ahnika could tell that Raj took great pleasure in dressing her in a traditional Zylan outfit, a style reserved for women who had been claimed by their mates. A male's sense of possessiveness calmed with knowing any who saw her dressed this way would understand she was taken. By him.

A brilliant violet color, the outfit had no waistband. It was made of individual pant legs gathered at the ankles and fastened to the side rings of the chains permanently encircling her waist. Her mating links wound through the skin around her waist and joined with the links going into her genitalia. She wore a strip of cloth draped over the front chain, pulled between her legs and wrapped over the back chain to hide her woman's hair. Her chest was covered with a short sleeveless vest, also in violet. The vest didn't close, but hung open over her breasts and ended right below her nipples, leaving the link chains between her nipples clearly visible.

But of course, *that* was the intent.

Ahnika sighed. She hated the outfit and yet she knew she was supposed to dress in the traditional mate garments for the rest of her life. Even if she didn't feel comfortable exposing her body this way. There wasn't anything she could do about it and the color *was* very pretty.

Raj dressed in the male version of Zylan traditional wear. Black pants with a waistband hitting him low on the hips, a horizontal slit in the material below his navel to highlight the link in his body. He wore a short tunic, which set off the links on his chest.

Seeing Nika gowned as his mate had a profound physical effect on him. It would be hard to control his growing erection and silently he acknowledged the need to revise his travel plans if this kept up.

With a wave of his hand, all trace of their presence vanished from the cavern. "Come to me, little love. I will shift us outside and we can begin our journey to Tanar." Enveloping her in his arms and using a thought, he took them back to the little cove. He scanned the area and marked the absence of any Hunters. *Good.* "My plan is to location-shift for most of the distance. We will have to make several hops, stopping to rest and scan for Hunters along the way. Just relax and let me hold you."

Nika did as she was told, allowing him to pick her up in his arms. Traveling this way would be disorienting so she closed her eyes and let him move them from place to place with his thoughts. Her own thoughts couldn't help but focus on the upcoming meeting in Tanar with Tar and Mica. Raj assured her that both men would have their mates present, giving her female support and so she could relay her story to all of them at one time. He'd filled the time when they weren't mating with stories of the two couples and they sounded like an interesting group of people.

Raj understood her social abilities were almost nonexistent after spending two life cycles alone. She had struggled since she escaped to feel comfortable with people again, but more than one or two strangers around her at a time made her nervous. Nika wasn't sure she would ever feel comfortable in large groups again. Smiling to herself, she realized it was horribly pathetic to think of six people as a large group.

Thinking of what was to come brought a whole new list of worries. Did Raj live in Tanar? Her pulse escalated in near panic. They hadn't spent any time talking about where they would live when this was over. She knew she couldn't handle living in a big city and all that it implied. It had been hard enough trying to cope with the press of humanity in the small outpost of Vidar. Goddess knows how she would handle the Ruling Place. It must be huge.

"Nika."

She really needed to talk to Raj about this. He had to know that she couldn't...

"My heart, what's wrong? Come on, love. Breathe. Everything will be okay," he murmured soothingly. She was scaring him, she'd grown stiff in his arms and he could feel her mounting tension through the links.

Nika turned wild eyes on Raj. She hadn't even realized they'd stopped. Watching her glance around in mild panic, through the links he felt her try to regain control over her fear.

"What is it, Nika? Do you sense danger nearby?" When she shook her head, he asked, "Does location shifting bother you?"

"No. It's not that," she replied softly. "I am sorry, Raj. I was just thinking about being in Tanar and all the people. I don't know if I can do this. I don't think I can take being around others for very long and I'm worried. Do you live in Tanar, Raj? I don't think I can live..."

She was doing it again. Her fear screamed down the links and into his heart. He held her tight to his chest and turned to sit on a log with Nika cradled on his lap. "It's okay, little one. It's okay. Breathe for me. In. Out. We will only be in Tanar a short time and you can stay in the Ruling Place if you wish, sequestered in my chambers there. You only have to see Tar and Mica and their mates."

He waited for her to relax and focus on him. "I don't live in Tanar, sweet, or in any large city. My family home is in Zelph. I live on the outer edge of the small village where there is a large lake and several streams nearby and a small pond on our property. It's a bit remote and there aren't many people in the area. You will be happy there. As your mate, I can do no less than make sure this is so."

Nika smiled at the smug confidence in his tone. But she was reassured that they would only be in Tanar for a short time. She could hide in his chamber if she needed to and he would understand and explain her phobia to others, as she didn't want to offend anyone by her need to be alone.

"Thank you, Raj, for understanding. I am sorry to be so..."

"Don't. Do *not* apologize for anything, Nika. I recognize how hard this is for you, what you have gone through. We will work through any issues together and make any changes necessary to make you feel safe and happy. Never hesitate to tell me if you are uncomfortable in a situation or need time alone. Well...not alone, but with only me," he said with an exaggerated leer.

Relieved, she laughed happily and ran her fingers through his dark hair. In the suns, his hair took on red highlights she hadn't noticed before they'd entered the cave and the feel of the soft strands were warm to her touch. "You are insatiable."

"Yeah, and we need to keep moving or I'll keep us here for another couple of *bi-nons*. This is a beautiful part of the forest, what do you say we walk for a while? I told Mica we would be at the palace shortly after dark and we have plenty of time to enjoy being outside and together."

"That would be nice. We were confined in the cave for a long time and while I enjoyed my time there, it would be wonderful to stretch my legs a bit."

Raj could strangle himself, knowing that her ordeal made her a little claustrophobic and yet he hadn't given her a chance to enjoy being out in the open. He swore he would remember to give her time each *bi-non* to enjoy the outdoors. After this conversation, he would watch to make sure she wasn't getting overwhelmed in any way. It would take time to heal the emotional scars from being in Brac's ghastly care.

He held her hand as they started walking down the trail. It was a beautiful day. The suns' rays cut through the trees and warmed their skin, creating patterns of light and shadow along the path. There were many flowers in bloom during this season and the blossoms created a vivid pattern of color against the aqua foliage of the forest. A light breeze blew, bringing with it the spicy fragrance of growing things.

"Raj, can I ask you a question?"

"Of course, my love. What bothers you? I can feel your confusion."

"Do you know how I can work on my psychic powers? I feel as if there are things locked inside me that are just waiting to pour out, but the power seems frozen inside. Or worse, I have an idea of what my abilities might be but I can't seem to fine-tune them enough to be useful. Like my premonition in Vidar, I could feel *something* coming closer, but I didn't know what or where it was coming from. It is very frustrating." Nika stopped and turned to look at Raj, her brow creased in agitation. He could tell this had been worrying her.

"Many psychic powers are discovered by accident. There are tests you can go through to uncover some of the more common abilities. I can help you try some of the simple exercises and Mica will be able to help you with the more complicated trials. You will also share some of my abilities now."

"Will they get stronger the more time I spend under Zylar's moons?"

"Yes. Definitely. Your powers will grow by leaps and bounds. Sometimes the power is there—it just takes using it to realize what you're dealing with. Like the premonitions, the more you have them…the more you will be able to understand what the apprehensiveness means to you."

Satisfied with his explanation, they continued to walk through the forest, often along trails too narrow for them to remain side by side and Raj let Nika take the lead. This was totally selfish on his part as he spent the time behind her fantasizing. He loved the effortless way she moved, the smooth and fluid motion of her body as she glided over the ground. He especially enjoyed watching the sway of her bottom and how the material between her legs would sometimes expose little bits of her skin or stretch tight across her buttocks to cuddle and frame her ass. Her hair was done in a long braid that swayed from side to side when she walked, mesmerizing him.

Strolling behind her, he thought how easy it would be to pull the fabric from between her thighs and have her open to him. He unconsciously clenched his hands into tight fists as he imagined sinking his fingers into her, kneading her bottom and pulling her tight against him. It was becoming almost impossible to walk, as with each step his cock seemed to grow and harden with its own demand. Unable to stop this sexual fantasy, he imagined draping her over a fallen log and driving into her over and over again. The sunlight would gleam over her skin and he'd watch himself sink into her depths.

He let his guard down and allowed her soul trails to reach back and stroke him. Opening their psychic link, he tugged on those glimmering threads at the same time.

"Raj?" Nika stopped and turned to him, her eyes heavy with passion. He used their connection to broadcast his longing for her, let her see his thoughts and the mental images of how they could pleasure one another. Their mating fervor still controlled much of their actions and he knew she would feel the pull and have no desire to fight against it. Aroused and hungry, he waited for her.

Silently she walked up to him and, without words, reached out to lightly run her hand down his chest and feather a brush of touch over his penis. Stroking against the sensitive head, she skimmed the long root through the fabric.

With a thought, Raj had them naked.

Plucking an intriguing picture from his mind, she slipped through his hands and lost no time in dropping to her knees in front of him to worship his body with her mouth. Hot and moist she slid over the tip, the sensation a tight fist of pleasure. Sucking in a breath as her tongue danced along his ultra-sensitive rim around the head of his shaft, and he exhaled as she sent waves of stimulation through his entire body.

His teeth clenched and every muscle tightened while his blood pounded hot in his veins. The links gathered energy and amplified the feelings back to them. The boundary between their thoughts shifted and blurred as each stroke of her mouth and tongue was shared within their collective consciousness.

The combination of savage lust and love hit them at the same time. Very little of his brain functioned and he could only focus on moving his hips to follow the rhythm she set. Fighting the urge to bury his hands in her hair and pull her closer, he instead set them on his hips, as he didn't wish her to think he was trying to force her to pleasure him. Pulling him deeper into her throat, she tantalized and tormented him until the pressure built to an unbearable degree. The links' connection swelled with the desires of Nika's body. This wouldn't be enough for him. He had to have the heat of her clenching sheath surrounding him.

Growling deep in his throat, he reached down to tug carefully at her hair and brought her face away from his groin. Looking up at him with her eyes glazed in a sensual fog, he forced her up his body and slid his hands over her.

Kneading her breasts, he played with the chains at her nipples and made her gasp and writhe in his hands. Bending his head to find her mouth, he tasted the salty essence of his pre-come on her tongue. Taking control of her body, he worked to ensure she caught up with his hunger. Nibbling at her mouth, he simultaneously opened her thighs with his leg and slid his hand over her stomach, stopping to tease the link chain at her belly button. She moaned into his mouth.

He continued down to the mass of tiny curls over her mound and found her dripping with moisture. She was ready for him. Wanting him. Sampling the hot, slick wetness by pushing two fingers into her channel, he ignored her cries of passion and pushed deeper, forcing her to ride his hand, wanting her to burn for him. She cried out his name, her breath coming in gasps.

Only when she begged him, as her body rocked and started to tighten around his fingers, did he look around to find the nearest log. Finding one a few feet away, he mentally fashioned a soft blanket to protect her soft skin and covered the bark. Gently positioning her, he bent her over the log so the curve of her bottom was at the perfect angle. Nika used her arms to hold her upper body away from the tree so she could look over her shoulder at him. The sun embellished her red skin with its golden caress and he saw heat flare in her eyes as he moved against her. Reveling in the sight of her spread before him, he palmed the flesh of her ass and rubbed his erection along the seam of her perfect cheeks.

Her pussy was hot and slick and he used the ripe head of his cock to nuzzle against it lovingly. She pushed back, trying to get him to enter her, but he held on, prolonging the *minon*, enjoying the friction and building the tormenting pulse of the links hum.

Enjoying the view as the tip of his shaft disappeared within the enveloping folds of her body until he could take no more. The first *minon* of full entry felt like heaven. He thrust hard, his hands on her hips as her tight sheath swallowed his shaft and her breasts swayed beneath her. Over and over he dove into her with long, fast strokes while she bucked and sobbed. Moving one hand along her back he reached around her to take a breast in his palm, pulling his fingers together to pinch the tip. He delighted in her scream.

Nothing mattered but the velvet friction and heat he found between her thighs. Linked without end and sharing sensations, he balanced on the brink of control. Feeling her need for more, he thrust deeper, used the shared mental path to move exactly the way she wanted him to. Dragging her back toward him with each hard stroke, he rode her hard and furiously, wanting to stay a part of her forever. She cried out in pleasure and rolled her hips to meet him.

They were wild and frantic, mating to try and fill the terrible hunger they carried embedded within their bodies for each other. He felt her body tighten around his, milking…demanding as she shattered with her release. With a loud roar, he poured his seed deep within her womb and slowly lowered his chest over her, carefully resting his head on her back while their hearts settled to the same rhythm and he rode the final vibrations of pleasure within her quivering flesh.

Chapter Nine

ഇ

Raj moved them to a nearby stream where they could wash and cool off in the water. After they dried, he once again dressed them in their link garments and then provided something to eat. He'd been constantly scanning the area and sensed no threat. It would be a good time for Nika to practice some of her powers. "Have you ever shifted your form before, Nika?"

She looked at him with a sad smile. "No. Before being captured, I had no idea of any of my psychic powers and there was no reason to try while I was alone in my cell. I never knew if I could transform or not."

"Transformation can be difficult and there are only a select few with this ability. It is one of my strongest powers, and with our link should be easy for you to accomplish now," he commented. "Our link bond will allow me to merge with your mind and project the steps you need to follow. Conversely, I will be here to assist you if you have any problems returning to your own form. The links will also enable us to communicate mentally no matter what form we are in. Would you like to try? We can travel most of the remaining distance in *leonar* form and still be in Tanar before the moons rise."

"Oh, yes! I would love to be able to transform. Tell me what to do!" she demanded, excitement evident in her glowing face.

Relieved to have found a way to take the sadness from her eyes, he stood and motioned her closer. "It will be easier if I show you." Creating a link with her mind, he mentally showed her, in easy steps, what she needed to do.

"Got it!" Exclaiming excitedly she closed her eyes, concentration creasing her brow. Zylar's *leonars* were a very large breed of feline with spotted gray-black fur. Her body shook with anticipation as she followed the instructions Raj provided. Soon, she blinked at his human form from the restless eyes of a large female cat. Mentally she giggled. *Come on, Raj. Let's run.*

Smiling, he dropped to the ground. The much larger body of the male *leonar* crowded impatiently into the smaller female as he lightly nipped the back of her neck. They padded away from the stream and were soon bounding through the woods.

Raj couldn't shake the thought that before they transferred back to their human form he would like to see if the story of sex with the *leonar's* barbed cock was as fantastic as the rumors and hints had led him to believe. It was purported the barb could keep them tied together for a very long time...even several *nilts*. If she were in heat, it would be *bi-nons* before they could break the connection.

Supposedly the barb would hit a spot within the female, causing an orgasm of mythical proportions. When they reached the outlying borders of Tanar, he would see how much time they'd used up. He realized the anticipation would keep him half-aroused for the remainder of the journey.

Nika was having more fun than she'd ever imagined. Running and leaping, soaring across the ground in the form of the *leonar* was an experience she would often want to repeat. The animal's senses gave her a different perspective of the world around her, allowing her to hear many things she wouldn't have noticed. In this form, she could hear bugs crawl along the ground and the whisper of soft wind high in the trees. The only problem with her new body seemed to be its constant state of semi-arousal. She'd been on low vibrate almost from the time they'd transformed.

The closer they got to their destination, the more pronounced the carnal sensations became. By the time Raj indicated they should stop, her body rippled with anxious alarm and the need to mate. The hidden links inside the beast's body seemed to stroke her from within and thrum straight through her center. Growling in agony, she rolled onto her back. *Raj!*

Nika's cat body burned with primal heat. Meeting the feral gaze of the beast who'd moved to stand over her, she hissed. Caging her with his body, his large paws straddled her form, his head bent to her neck and he bared his teeth against her throat. Her animal heart thrilled in reaction to his domineering position as she recognized her mate.

Mine. You need me, Nika. You need me, now! You are mine in all ways. I have claimed you. You burn for what only I — and my cock — can give you. In the last throes of linking fever, Raj realized their thoughts had become entwined with the beasts. It didn't matter if the three moons of Zylar were rising and Mica expected them in Tanar, they could not deny this.

Okay. Can't concentrate...help me change...

No! This way. Let me bury this cock deep within you. I can't wait, Nika. Now! Raj nuzzled Nika's exposed neck and lowered his body to push his unsheathed cock against her furry stomach. Letting her feel the hot pulsing need he could no longer control, he rubbed against her and purred into her softness while he vibrated the open links to share his spiraling arousal. Shifting to the side, he rolled her to her stomach by butting against her with his head. Once she'd gained her feet, he bit the back of her neck and forced her to drop to her front paws and raise her hips. Positioning his large body over her smaller form, he situated his groin against her exposed flanks.

Pushing the swollen head of his cock against her wild heat, he growled low in his throat in reaction to the sensitive barb breaking through the tip of his flesh. Exploring the responsive area exposed to him, he raked the barb over her inflamed tissues...but didn't penetrate. Moving and sliding against her, he pulled away before he could find a home in her weeping sheath.

Growling her displeasure, she pushed back against him but he avoided her, moving away. Again she pressed in urgent demand, this time using her mind to punctuate her need. *Now. Do it now!* The link between them allowed him to feel her growing desperation...the throbbing spiral of ache deep inside her. With a hard forward thrust, he plunged into her body and then rocked from the devastating reaction as the barb burst fully through his skin and lodged in her inner folds.

Ahnika roared in primal ecstasy at the piercing jolt when something stabbed into an unknown spot deep within her. The sharp pleasure-pain sent her into a mindless fervor. The added movement of fur-covered balls slapping against an outside pleasure point combined to drive her body to a clawing desperation.

His haunches worked against her, pumping furiously as she arched into the pleasure, meeting every thrust. Using the links, he magnified every sensation and when her climax built and then burst around him, he demanded more. Driving her to the brink over and over again, he allowed her to fall and then worked them both to an even higher peak. He continued to assault her senses, forcing her beyond the limits of her human endurance. Beyond the limits of his own as he permitted the beast to take over with his barbed cock buried in his mate's passage—no longer able to control the animal within.

Each time she came, it was as if the world exploded and all feeling in the universe existed within her small frame. It would slam through her and she would be certain she would die from too much pleasure and before she could collapse, he would be pushing her up again. His body surrounded her. His cock, so thick and hot, filled her...stroking desperately inside until the barbed jolts threatened to tear her apart.

And, linked, he rode every wave with her, feeling blast after blast of explosive energy. Her body began to vibrate with intense eruptions. The orgasms were strung like beads, one following another with no rest in between the showers of exquisite release erupting through them. The pleasure built so high, it shot them hurtling into a climatic detonation that ripped them into unconsciousness. Their bodies remained connected and they twitched in silent oblivion with the aftershocks.

* * * * *

Using mind-speak, Raj called to Mica as he shifted into his chambers at the Ruling Place holding his sleeping mate in his arms.

You're later than you planned. Was there any trouble? Mica thought the words with concern.

No trouble, just... Raj could hear his brother's chuckle in his mind.

No need to explain, I still have a hard time focusing on things other than my mate. I do not think I can keep Nyssa and Tala from storming into your chamber, however. The little patience those two have has worn thin, he warned.

We will come meet you in a minon. *Mica, warn the others. Nika's experience with Brac has left it difficult for her to be in an enclosed space with other people for any length of time. Her body has healed but her mind still needs time to deal with some things. She would want them to know she means no disrespect if we need to leave quickly.*

Mica was silent for an extended time. *I, too, am anxious to hear your mate's story. You say her body is healed. Do you want me to examine her to make sure?* he offered.

No. She is fine. Maybe in a few bi-nons, *when she is comfortable with you, she would allow you to check her for any lingering effects.*

When I see her this evening, I will scan her to make sure there isn't anything to worry about. Is that okay with you?

Raj sighed. He knew his brother, it didn't matter if it was all right with him or not, Mica would do it to make sure if anything were wrong, they would find it immediately.

Again Mica's deep laughter rumbled in his mind. *You are right. How silly of me to ask. We will be waiting for you in Tar's chamber.*

I get the message. We will be there soon.

Raj put Ahnika on the bed and said softly, "Nika, wake up, sweet love."

She opened her eyes and smiled at her mate. "Sorry, Raj. I just needed a little *cat*nap."

"Ha. Ha. Don't remind me, baby. The others are waiting for us and we are out of time. Let me brush your hair back and I will get us some clean clothes and we can go join them."

"Yes, it is time. I feel guilty for leaving the other women at Brac's mercy since I've been gone."

"You have nothing to feel guilty about. All of the guilt should belong to Brac. We will just have to make sure he pays for it."

He lovingly brushed her hair and they both freshened up. They walked solemnly to Tar and Nyssa's chambers holding hands. Ahnika took a deep breath before they stepped inside.

The first and only thing she noticed as they stepped into the chamber were the two very large men standing across the room. *Oh, Goddess help me*, she thought. Both men were huge, yet one man towered over the other. The tallest, scariest-looking man had black hair with bright copper highlights. *His hair looks very similar to Brac's*. Nika shuddered.

This man had muscles on his muscles and seemed to ooze psychic power. "I can't do this," she mumbled. And then he turned to look at her with Raj's ice-blue eyes and a feeling of peace and comfort washed over her. With the calm, came the ability to look at him more carefully. In his hair, the copper highlights were vibrant and alive, not the dull sheen she'd noticed in Brac's hair. *This is Mica.* Taking a deep breath she relaxed marginally and shifted her gaze to the other man.

This must be Tar. His muscles were a little subtler and he had curly dark blue-black hair and silver eyes. If he hadn't been standing close to the giant next to him, he would have been intimidating. This was Zylar's Ruler and for two life cycles, she had thought he'd been responsible for her nightmare. Once again she started to tense when Raj whispered softly in her ear.

"It's okay, Nika," he said soothingly.

She could feel him using the links as he tried to soothe her nerves. Turning to look at him, she knew her eyes must be a little wild so she worked hard to control her fear.

"Nika, this is VaNyssa, Tar's mate. And, Tala, Mica's tormentor," he introduced her to the women, trying to take her attention away from the two imposing males.

"He only calls me that because it's true," Tala laughed. "Welcome, little sister. I am so happy to meet you." Tala was thinking the same thing everyone in the room tried to process. Here was a beautiful woman that someone had hurt.

And hurt badly. Raj's new mate was all long, shimmering hair, glorious red skin and big, frightened eyes.

Nika frowned when she looked at the women. "I don't understand, you are both mated but what are you wearing?" Her eyes got even bigger and she slapped her hand over her mouth. Quickly she apologized, "I am sorry, that was terribly rude."

Nyssa giggled. "No, it wasn't and call me Nyssa. I am very happy to meet you, Nika. Tala and I are wearing jeans and tee shirts—clothes from Earth. I refuse to wear the Zylan equivalent of a harem sex fantasy unless I absolutely have to. Tala has started doing the same. Once I figured out how to manufacture clothes from thin air and figured out hip-huggers didn't irritate the mating links, it was goodbye to *I Dream of Jeanie*. The only time we dress in traditional-chain-sex-wear is if there is a formal state function and it won't be long before I change that!"

"Nyssa," Tar growled in warning.

Nika looked thoroughly confused and Tala took pity on her saying, "Don't even try and figure out most of what she just said. I have been listening to her for *setnons* and she still makes my head hurt. You just have to concentrate on what you understand and let her babble about the rest."

Tar snorted and Nyssa just smiled and stuck her tongue out at her mate. "Okay...now I am sorry to have confused you. You look very pretty, Nika."

"I hate these clothes," Nika snarled. She turned to Raj. "Please, make me some of those...whatever they are."

"You hate your clothes? Nika, why—"

"I hate them!" she said vehemently. "They make me feel as if everyone is looking at me in a way I don't want them to and they can see the scars on my back if my hair isn't down and..." She stopped, horrified at what she'd just said.

Raj closed his eyes and groaned inwardly at his stupidity. Before he had a chance to comfort her, Nyssa and Tala pulled her away from him.

"We will be right back. I have the hang of this now and can get Nika dressed in something more comfortable in a flash. Tar, honey, please blink everybody up something to drink. Preferably something with alcohol...I think they're all going to need it. Nika, would you like pants or would you prefer a simple dress that covers more than the handkerchief you're wearing?" she asked as they left the room.

Tala murmured quietly, "If your back is still sore, the dress will be more comfortable. These jeans take a little getting used to. It's the strangest thing, but the more you wear them the more you can't do without..." As they moved further away, their voices trailed off.

Raj looked at Mica and Tar. "I am going to kill Brac," he stated flatly.

"I have a feeling we are all going to feel the same way," Tar said. Before he could question Raj, the women came back into the room.

Standing between Tala and Nyssa was a beaming Nika. Dressed simply in a loose aqua-colored gown shirred a little at her breast, the neckline was modest, only hinting at the full curves beneath. The skirt had no waistline, falling in tiny pleats from under her breast line to mid-calf. She'd taken her half boots off and gone barefoot like the other two women. She looked beautiful in the dress with her hair now arranged in a long braid slung over one shoulder. Raj realized she really had been using her hair as a sort of shield.

"Raj," she said excitedly. "Isn't it wonderful? I feel so much better dressed this way. Is it okay? You don't really mind, do you?"

He smiled at her. How could he mind when it meant so much to her? He would do anything for his mate. "It looks gorgeous, Nika, and I definitely don't mind. We will work with Nyssa to find the styles and types of clothing you like and I will learn how to fashion them for you."

Tar moved carefully across the room to his mate. He and Mica had decided if they sat as couples, it might put Nika at ease. "Well, let's all take a seat. As ordered by my loving mate, I have provided refreshments. And, Nyssa, my little pregnant cat, here is some of Zylan's best fruit juice," he said as he sat. Everyone got a drink and sat either on the low couch or on the vibrant red and green cushions on the floor.

Except for Nika who waved her hand at Raj and shook her head. "I don't think I can sit or drink anything. I want to just tell all of you what happened to me and get it over with. I would feel better standing here. Raj, you sit too." She didn't have long to wait before they were all settled with their eyes focused on her. Taking a deep breath she began her story.

"Two life cycles ago, I was kidnapped from my home planet of Zmar. I was with several other women and the men who took us were wearing tunics with the Zylan Royal Crest, Tar."

"What!" Tar exclaimed as he jumped to his feet. When he saw the distress on Nika's face, he quickly resumed his seat.

"It gets worse. Go on, baby, we will hold our questions until you get through it," Raj said softly.

Nika closed her eyes for a *minon* before she could go on. "I woke up in a small underground cell where I was kept locked in and alone for almost one life cycle. I was allowed out only to bathe once every other *bi-non* or so. It was dark and quiet, except for during the nights. At night, I could hear other women crying. Sometimes there was screaming. Earlier this life cycle, my captors broke the routine and I was brought out of my room by a guard to meet another man. His hair was almost the same color as yours," she said, pointing at Mica. "I learned after I escaped his name was Brac. The guard remained in the room along with a woman. He — Brac — told me the reason I had been kidnapped was to be sold to another man as a mate," she paused and swallowed. If she could just get through this next part, Raj could take over.

Looking at all of them in turn, they seemed to be biting their tongues, impatient to ask questions with anger and shock evident on their faces.

"There is more. Brac made the woman disrobe and he showed me her mating links. These links weren't real — he'd made them and they could be controlled with a small black box. The black box sent varying levels of pain through the links. He demonstrated by causing that poor woman pain and then he forced her to pleasure the guard." Nika had to stop again and wait for the exclamations to die down. Unable to look them in the eye for this part, she concentrated on a spot over their heads and resolutely went on.

"I was to be trained in sexual submission like all the other women he kept locked in. Only I refused to cooperate. They tried to make me...do things to men they brought in and, when I refused, I was beaten or whipped. That is why my back is scarred," her voice trembled.

"Oh, Nika," Nyssa and Tala moved as one, wanting to comfort her.

"Don't!" she cried and held out her hands. "I'll never finish this if I don't get it all out now and if you touch me, I'll cry."

They sat back down, this time holding tightly to their mates. Raj sat alone, jaw and hands clenched in anger. He kept his mind closed tight, not wanting to add his feelings to Nika's already overwhelmed emotions.

"I escaped the night before they were to implant my links. They made me watch this process with others and it was a painful, bloody and horrific procedure. The healers

Brac used didn't just thread the metal through their bodies — there is some kind of psychic attachment created so the contraption can't be removed. They were so sure once the links were in place I wouldn't be able to resist their commands or *training*," she spat out. "I knew I had to get away from there by either running or forcing them to kill me. I was lucky to escape and even luckier when Raj found me after the other Hunters grabbed me in Vidar's marketplace. I think Raj can fill you in on some of the rest of it and if I can just have a few *minons*, I think I will be able to answer questions," she said as she turned and ran for the bathing room in the inner chamber. She was going to be sick and she didn't want to embarrass herself.

Raj moved to follow her. "Tala and I will go, Raj," Nyssa said. "Let us give her a sister's comfort. If we need you, we will call but you had better stay here and tell Mica and Tar how you think we can kill this son of a bitch!" Nyssa and Tala ran after Nika and he started to follow anyway.

"Nyssa is right, Raj. Let them hold her while she is sick. Women often will try to be strong with their mates, not wanting to worry us. Let her use their shoulders to cry on. If I know Nyssa and Tala, they will comfort her, get a little more of the details from her and then band together like the militant females they are — to storm Brac's fortress," Mica said quietly.

"Nika isn't going anywhere near him," Raj stated between clenched teeth.

Mica sighed. "Yeah, I can understand your feeling that way. And because you are newly mated, you actually believe you can keep her from being involved. Tar and I will try our best to keep all three of the women out of it, but I wouldn't want to bet on the final outcome."

Tar just grunted.

Raj shook his head. "Nika would never go against my wishes."

This time both Tar and Mica laughed at him.

"Oh, brother…I hope I am around when you realize the ludicrousness of your statement. Now, first I want to tell you I scanned Nika and she seems to be in good health. I sense no infection or any injury so, Raj, you don't need to worry about her physical condition. Will you fill us in on your meeting with Brac and what you have discovered about this mess?" Mica demanded.

Raj was pleased to know Nika carried no lasting injuries. Before he could answer Mica's question, Tar started pacing the room like a caged animal.

Tar couldn't sit still. "I can't even get my mind around what questions to ask you, Raj. I am so…shocked and disgusted. Angry. I hurt for Nika and I don't even want to contemplate how many other women are out there that he's done this to."

"There are a lot of them, Tar. She didn't even get to the part about the auctions."

"Auctions!" both Tar and Mica exclaimed.

"Auctions," Raj said tonelessly. "I believe about every other *setnon*, Brac would auction off a few women to the highest bidder. He would strip the women and let the invited men fondle their bodies and torture them with pain from the little black boxes. Then these men would bid on the captive women. Brac made the others like Nika, watch so they would be 'prepared' for their time. We know he has been doing this for at least as long as the two life cycles Nika was held captive. But, Tar, I think it is worse. Nika said there had been rumors about the Zylan Ruler being involved in slaving raids for many additional life cycles before she was taken. If this is true, then we are looking at the possibility of more than fifty women who have been sold into sexual slavery over the last four or five life cycles."

Tar couldn't hold his anger in. He roared and bent to pick up the low table in front of him and threw it against the wall. Crazed at the thought these vile acts were not only being committed, but done in his name, he started for the door ready to tear Brac into small pieces with his own hands. Mica and Raj had to physically restrain him from leaving the room.

"I know, Tar. I have been battling the same urge since the *minon* Ahnika told me what happened," Raj said quietly.

Mica laid a hand on each of their shoulders. "What we need to do is finish this, and I do not want to wait very long to do so. Tar, you and I need to sit and listen while Raj tells us everything he knows and then, when our mates come back in to the room, we will need to ask our questions and come up with a plan. Brac has been hiding this from us for a long time. He has to be smarter than he looks so we need to plan our strategy well." With the calm voice of reason, Mica encouraged them to sit down and listen to Raj as he finished telling the story.

Chapter Ten

✿

Ahnika groaned, embarrassed to have Nyssa holding her hair out of the way while she dry-heaved. Tala placed a cool wet cloth at the base of her neck and she'd flash-lit incense when she came in the room. It had helped. The light floral scent was calming and just the presence of the two women seemed to be helping her relax and let her push her churning emotions away. Still feeling stretched to her limit, the memories were no longer making her physically ill.

"Why don't we all jump in the small bathing pool? I had Tar make some adjustments to it so it will bubble around us and the warm water will be soothing. We can have a drink and just relax and take some time to get to know each other." Nyssa said softly. At Nika's blank look and Tala's frown, she smiled. "It's an Earth thing…trust me on this. We called it a Jacuzzi and it is very comforting. We don't have to be naked…I'll just—"

Nyssa waived her hand and all three women were clothed in bikinis with their hair piled loosely on top of their heads. "—provide the swimsuits and the wine for you two and—come on…trust me—just get in and unwind. I promise you we will all feel better after a quick soak." She laughed at the women's confusion with their attire as she guided Nika down the steps. Tala followed.

The women sat in comfortable silence for a *minon*, enjoying the swirling warm water. Nika felt her muscles relax and she was surprised to find she did feel better, felt more in control of her tumultuous emotions.

"I am going to ignore these very strange triangles of cloth and just assume you know what you are doing, Nyssa," Tala mumbled. "So, Nika, you are from Zmar. Do you have family there?" she asked brightly.

Nika blinked. She guessed she would ignore Nyssa's strange ways as well as it seemed the only way to deal with the eccentric woman. "I did when I left. My mother and father and two brothers live there. I haven't wanted to think about what they have been going through," she said miserably.

"We will talk to Tar and Mica as soon as we are ready and see if there isn't some way to get word to your family. You'll want to invite them to Zylar for the claiming ceremony," Tala replied.

Nika blanched, she hadn't thought about the claiming ceremony.

"Don't look like that, Nika. Nyssa has managed to make some very major changes to the ceremony. You no longer have to be brought to sexual peak with the links in front of anyone. When it came time for her ceremony, Nyssa turned the tables on Tar and used the links to make him orgasm in front of the Council of Ten, which proved to everyone that women could use the links just like the men have always been able to. Those actions started a revolution of sorts. The end result of her escapade is that on Zylar drawing on the links for the claiming ceremony has been dropped," Tala stated smugly.

Nika frowned, she remembered Raj saying something about this, but she hadn't questioned it at the time. "What do you mean Nyssa used the links? I thought only men—"

Nyssa snorted inelegantly and took a sip of her juice. "Of course you thought only men could use the links. In their male smugness, they assumed the all-powerful men would be the only ones who could use them, but it's not the truth.

Women can use them just as well but evidently no one ever bothered to try. When Tar tried to control me with sex, and granted it was mind-blowing sex, I didn't know I wasn't supposed to be able to use them on him." She shrugged. "But I did. On Earth, men and women are considered equal. Anything they can do, we can do. Just remember this when Raj is trying to manipulate you with screaming orgasms. You have a brain and you can use the links to persuade him to your way of thinking."

"Raj would never try to use sex to manipulate me," Nika said indignantly. "And you did this in front of the Ruling Council?"

Tala snorted. "You just wait until you want to do something Raj doesn't want you to do, then tell us again how he won't use the links."

"Just always remember, you have control of the links as well… Don't let Raj go all macho on you. And yeah, I used the links in front of the Ruling Council. It caused more than a little friction. Since then, I have met with every one of the Ten's mates, and several hundred other women who have heard what happened. The reaction is mixed. People are either ecstatic about the changes, or they've decided I'm Satan." Nyssa smirked.

"Except for Brac's mate," Tala said softly.

Nyssa looked at Tala questioningly and then nodded. "I met with all the mates of the Ten, except for Brac's," she agreed. "I hadn't even realized she didn't seek me out."

Nika heaved a sigh. "I think things make more sense now. Well, not sense but I understand something Brac said. When he demonstrated the links to me that horrible night, he started raving about how the links were never enough to keep the women in line, and a man needed more control. Then he segued into ranting how recently the lack of control became even worse. How certain women really didn't know their place. Women who thought they had a right to use the links and made no attempt to submit to their husbands. I didn't have a clue what he was talking about."

This time it was Nyssa who turned pale. "Oh My God! He has been doing this because—"

"Don't even think it, Nyssa," Tala snapped. "You have only been on Zylar for less than a life cycle. Brac has been doing this to women for way longer than that—he kidnapped Nika before you even got to Zylar. You are not to blame."

"No," Nika agreed. "Brac is solely responsible for this mess. Which brings up another concern—not only do we have to get the women away who are in the fortress now, but he has been doing this for so long, we need to find the women he has sold at auction and rescue them as well. We can't leave anyone in his power. And there is one more thing I forgot to mention before." Nika tried to gather her thoughts. She wanted to make sure they would understand what she was trying to say.

"When I first met Brac, he asked me if I knew what links were."

"Why did he do that? Zmarians have links just like...oh dear Goddess!" Tala paled.

"What? What am I missing? Why are you both so upset that Brac asked Nika what a link is?" Nyssa looked confused.

"Because any planet close enough for space travel already has the links. It would be a very stupid question to ask unless Brac—or someone who works for him—has the ability to sift space as Mica did to send Tar to you and bring you both back to Zylar," Tala said.

"I'm not sure I understood all of what you were saying, Tala. But my point is some of the women come from planets that don't have mating links. Which means Brac's abduction and subsequent enslavement will be even more of a shock to them. The magnitude of his evil actions just seems to grow the more we think about it." Nika sighed heavily.

All three women paused and thought about the ramifications of the women out there living a life of cruel subjugation. Nyssa wondered if some of the women could possibly be from Earth. Her reaction to finding herself on Zylar was bad enough—she could imagine how horrible it would have been without having a true mate, and the kindness of people like Tala and Mica to make the transition easier. Add Brac's depravity to the mix and the experience would have been pure hell.

"Are you feeling better, Nika? I think maybe it's time to join the guys and discuss the rest of this as a group so we can come up with a plan. I hate the thought of waiting any longer to liberate those poor women." Nyssa didn't wait for Nika's assurance, no matter what Tala said, she felt like Brac did this because of her actions since she came to Tanar.

The women dried and dressed and then walked into the room to see all three men pacing.

As soon as the women entered the room, each man moved straight to his mate and took them in their arms. Each of them felt the need to touch their mates and thank the Goddess for each other and for the bonds they'd forged without the taint and misery Brac had created. The thought of all those women in peril made them realize how lucky they were.

"Tar, we need to figure out some way of letting Ahnika's family know she is safe," Nyssa said quietly as she pulled back from his embrace.

Raj started at Nyssa's comment, realizing that, once again, he hadn't even considered Nika's concern for the family she'd left behind. "Nika, love, did your family have a com device in their home?"

Nika looked at Raj, her eyes swimming with unshed tears. "Yes, my father is Chancellor of southern Zmar. Oh, Raj...can I try and get a hold of them now? I don't know the time difference, but my father was used to being summoned at any *nilt* for messages. Please?"

Wanting to make up for his thoughtlessness, he would give her anything in his power. He hadn't even asked about Nika's family, didn't know her father was Chancellor or that she had siblings. The only excuse he could come up with was the huge shock he'd experienced when he found his mental thoughts were taken over by the mating frenzy. "Of course you can call them, little one. Tar has a com device in this room we can use. Tar, do you have the coordinates for..." he trailed off and looked at Nika. "What is your father's name, baby?" he asked softly.

But this time it was Tar who answered. "His name is Ragnor and now his thinly veiled animosity toward me makes sense," he said disgustedly. "I am sure he thinks I had something to do with his daughter's disappearance. By Zylar's Moons, I will make Brac pay dearly for the abomination he has done to the women and for slandering my character!"

"What is a Chancellor?" Nyssa asked the room in general.

Mica answered, "It would be something like a vice-president for your America, Nyssa. Ragnor is responsible for governing a specific region in Zmar under their Ruler."

Nika and Raj walked over to the com unit while the rest of the group moved to the other end of the room to give them some privacy. They all watched intently as Nika and Raj spoke first to a tall, distinguished-looking gentleman and then an older version of Nika, a woman who couldn't stop crying. Brief explanations were made and assurances given that her parents and brothers would come to Zylar in the next couple of *bi-nons*. When they finished talking, Ragnor asked to speak to Tar for a *minon*.

Ragnor humbly apologized for his suspicions of Tar and offered his planet's support in dealing with Brac and the aftermath. Telling Tar he was authorized to speak for the Zmarian Ruler in this, Ragnor knew there would be no question in helping with any action needed against Brac. There was a reported twenty-five women who had been stolen from different areas on Zmar over the past several life cycles. Ragnor assured Tar the Zmarian people would be happy to assist in any recovery missions.

After the call, the mood in the room was somber and intense. Mica broke the contemplative silence. "We need to finish this," he stated gravely.

* * * * *

"Besides rescuing the women who are currently being held in Brac's fortress, we also need to find all those women who have been sold as well. How will we manage to find all of them?" Nyssa asked.

Nika frowned and replied, "When I was forced to attend the auction, I noticed when one of the men made a selection, Brac gave them some papers to sign. I am sure he kept them. If we could find the papers, we might be able to trace the other women."

"Yeah, and those papers will be the first thing Brac tries to destroy if we don't get to him first," Tala said.

"Nika, do you have any idea how many women are currently in the cells?" Mica asked.

Nika shook her head. "I can tell you there are ten doors, five on each side of the hall which looked the same as mine. The doors to the 'torture and training' rooms were larger and more ornate. I don't know if all the cells are occupied or if someone new was put in my cell," she stated.

"I know how we can find out how many women are there and maybe find the papers," Tala said.

"*No!*" Mica growled. "I will not allow it, Tala."

Tala shrugged. "I won't be in any danger because no one will see me or sense me. Even you don't know when I am in the same room with you when I use far-sight."

Raj looked at his brother in confusion. "What is she talking about, Mica?" he questioned.

"Tala has an unusual ability to project. The projection causes her body to just, well…evaporate. When her body disappears, she *becomes* her thoughts. I don't like her to do it because we haven't been able to figure out where her body goes when she uses this power. She doesn't take her body with her, nor does it remain behind like when we soul-shift. It just *disappears* while she's gone and she sends her mind wherever she wants it to go. She can see, hear and feel things when she gets there," Mica growled unhappily.

"Yes, and I will be able to wander around Brac's fortress without being seen, count the women in the cells as I can go through walls, and I might be able to find where he keeps the papers on the women. I could also figure out how many guards he has and see if he has any other defenses set up. If we don't know what we are getting into, or where things are, it puts us all at risk. What if Brac has moved everyone to another location? If he doesn't know Ahnika is with Raj, he has to know none of the Hunters have been able to find her. Wouldn't he be making plans in case she confides in someone?" Tala argued.

"Raj and I can transport into the fortress and do the same thing," Mica reasoned.

"Yes, you could. But when you transport, you take your body with you and you could be seen. If you were seen, it would alert Brac to the fact we know what he is doing. And if he has psychically shielded any areas, you would either set off his alarms or not be allowed to see what he has shielded. So far we know psychic shields have not affected my far-sight. We need the element of surprise if at all possible," she tried to persuade her mate.

Raj interjected, "Brac does have psychic shielding. I tried several times to soul-shift in order to try and find out what was going on. I couldn't get in."

"I don't like this, Tala," Mica grumbled.

"I don't like any of this, but we need to use the resources we have, Mica. It won't harm me. If I need you…if I get into any trouble…you know I can call to you and you can help me back. We practiced having you doing that, Mica, and we know it works," she stated eagerly.

Mica growled low in his throat, he did not want his mate anywhere near the fortress and Brac's evil, but he knew she was right. Maybe if he let her do this, she would stay out of the rescue itself. Knowing it was wishful thinking—he decided the bargain was worth a try. "If I allow you to do this, will you promise me it is the only part you will play in this rescue?" he asked.

Tala laughed. "Nice try. No, I won't promise you. We don't know what resources we will need to accomplish the rescue and I will not tie myself to any promise I might have to break. I *will* promise to be very careful, Mica. I do not want to end up in Brac's hands," she acknowledged carefully. "We should do it now. It is very late and I would imagine there are fewer bodies moving around the fortress at this time. If I go when the suns are up, the women could be out of their cells and would be harder to count. The guards could also be away from the fortress in the morning. Let me do this now," she pleaded.

The room stayed silent as they all watched Mica pace and run his hands through his hair, his displeasure obvious. "I hate this, Tala. But you are right…it needs to be done. Raj and Nika, if you would draw a map of what you each know of the fortress, Tala can look at it and get some idea of where she needs to go. Tala, why not take this time to meditate and prepare? I am going to transport outside of Brac's fortress for a *minon* and see if I can sense any psychic traps as well as look at the setup." With the stark pronouncement, Mica disappeared.

Nyssa provided paper and writing instruments for Raj and Nika and then left them to their tasks. Looking for her mate, she found Tar standing outside in their private garden looking up at the clear night sky. The three moons of Zylar hung bright and beautiful in the heavens. The night air was filled with the spicy-sweet scent of moonflower blossoms. When she'd first been brought to Zylar, she'd missed Earth so much. Now she couldn't imagine living anywhere else. This was her home. Her mate. Wrapping her arms around his stomach, she pressed her chest along his back. "We will get through this, Tar," she whispered softly.

He sighed and covered her arms with his own, taking comfort in his mate's closeness. "This is such a huge and horrifying mess, Nyssa. It is going to take so much time to retrieve all the women, not just from Brac's fortress... I know the rescue mission will happen soon. But the time it will take to find all the women he has taken and sold upsets me. I want every one of them found as quickly as possible. I can't bear the thought of them spending one *bi-non* they don't have to in captivity and pain." Hanging his head, he moaned. "It seems so petty of me to worry about the damage to my reputation. You know there are more planets and people out there who believe I had a part in this. Just as Ahnika's father, Ragnor, thought me responsible."

"I know, love. And I have some ideas on all of this. I think it would be a good idea to set up groups of Hunters and healers to search for the women. Groups of both women and men," she said.

Tar turned in his arms to look at Nyssa with a question in his eyes.

"When women have been traumatized by rape and violence, they will not be happy to have another man around them without a woman to act as a sort of buffer. They will need healing, not only physically but also mentally. My suggestion for recovering the women would be several Hunter-warriors and a couple of Selven goddesses to act as healers for each group. If you have several groups out looking for the women, they will be recovered much faster. Then, I think the recovered women should be encouraged to stay with the Selven for some intensive healing. You know they are going to need to have the false chains removed and they will benefit from some serious therapy."

Tar looked at his link-mate in amazement. "Good idea, little cat. Do you want to contact Shalan in the morning and explain what is going on here and get her approval to bring the women to the Refuge?" This sharing of thoughts and responsibilities was a new concept for him. He was learning how to work with his mate as a true partner and just beginning to see the many advantages to having a female point of view.

"I will. Shalan should come here as soon as possible. Once the women are rescued they will need to have their most serious injuries treated at the palace first. They will also need to rest and recuperate a bit before making the several days journey to the Refuge," she replied. "I also think we should take a few diplomatic trips."

"Diplomatic trips?"

"Tar, we don't know how involved this is. If all goes well, we'll uncover the documentation telling us who bought women, who participated in this obscene service of Brac's. Maybe it is his project and his project alone. But I am afraid we will find other high-ranking officials have also been involved. Nika told me earlier Brac ranted and raved about women who didn't know their place, women who thought they had a right to use the links and made no attempt to submit to their husband's demands. We know he has been undermining many of the changes you and I have been trying to make concerning the place of women on Zylar. We also know others believe you had a hand in this evil. We need to be honest and forthcoming about what happened here, reveal who was involved and what steps you and the Zylan council are going to take to undo the damage. Ahnika also said Brac had asked her if she knew what mating links were. Tala thinks this means either Brac or someone working with him are able to do some sort of planet sifting thing."

Nyssa sighed. "This whole rotten setup is a mess," she stressed. "But we need to face it head-on and make sure something like this never happens again and that everyone, everywhere understands we had no part in it."

Tar shook his head and asked, "How is it you have thought through all of this so quickly? I am just beginning to get my mind around the ramifications and all the horrid tendrils of far-reaching consequences?"

Nyssa snorted in disbelief. "I am from Earth. Political intrigue and serial madness are commonplace where I come from. I've never been involved in cleaning up such a nightmare, but I've seen damage control done many times. What we need to do is prepare for the worst that could happen and hope this situation falls far short of a universal plot to overthrow your government," she stated.

Tar shuddered and closed his eyes. Put that way, he had the horrible premonition Brac's activities were the tip of the proverbial Earth iceberg.

* * * * *

Mica returned to report he could sense no unusual psychic shielding over Brac's fortress and that all appeared to be quiet. Tala should have no trouble getting inside. Raj had drawn up a map of what he knew about Brac's upper levels and the way to the underground tunnels containing the hallway with the holding cells. Nika had added her input and drawn a map of the cells and the other rooms in the corridor she'd been kept in.

After some discussion, it was decided Tala would start underground and count the women and guards and then work her way upstairs to see if she could discover where Brac kept his paperwork.

The lights in the chamber were dimmed and protective candles lit. The soothing sweet scent would increase Tala's safety and energy. Tala made herself comfortable, lying on her back amid pillows on the floor. Closing her eyes, she thought of the entrance to the underground hallway in Brac's fortress. Picturing it in her mind, she projected her thoughts and awareness outward.

She didn't hear the gasps coming from the group gathered around her, or see the look of concern on her mate's face. What she saw was a dimly lit corridor with two burly guards stationed at the entrance. Cloaked deep in shadow, neither of the men moved as much as an inch when she brushed by them. She hurried by the common rooms, taking only enough time to reassure herself no one was within, she planned to enter each of the holding cells to count the women and see if she could sense what condition they were in. Then she would go upstairs and see what else she could find out about this place. It gave her the creeps.

To Tala, it seemed like she'd been gone only a few *minons*. But when she reappeared in the chamber at the Ruling Place, she could tell for those waiting for her return, the time had stretched immeasurably. Looking around at the drawn faces, she tried to smile triumphantly when her face was smothered against a broad shoulder as Mica tugged her into his arms.

"I hate it when you do this!" he exclaimed.

Tala moved her hand up to cup his face and gave him a quick kiss. "I know, love, you hate it because we don't yet understand it, but you can see I am fine and let me tell you, it was worth it. If I could just have a little something to drink, I will tell you what I found," she said hoarsely. For some reason, she always came back from her travels with a raspy voice.

Nyssa scrambled to get Tala a drink and Mica settled her more comfortably in his lap. He was not ready to let her move away from him. Tala took a couple of swallows of Zylan wine to soothe her parched throat and sighed.

"There are six women locked in the underground cells," she started. "Three have chains already attached to their bodies." She hesitated and then said sadly, "One woman has recently been beaten, she seemed badly bruised but I couldn't sense any broken bones or internal injuries. Pass me the map and I will mark which cells are occupied." Tala made the marks for the women on the map then made several additional marks and continued, "There are two large guards armed with flash wands and knives at the hallway entrance, here...and another two at the top of the stairs to the upper levels." She pointed to their locations on the map.

"What are flash wands?" Nyssa questioned.

"Umm, hard to explain. I don't think Earth has anything like them yet. Flash wands were created as a psychic weapon that can be used to fling bolts of pain and restrict movement. Depending on the mental capacity of the user, they can even cause death," Tar explained solemnly.

Nyssa sighed. "May the force be with you, Obi-Wan," she muttered.

"Don't ask," Tala hurriedly added as Nika started to question Nyssa's comment. "We'll be here all night."

"Did you get through any of the upper levels, Tala?" Mica questioned.

Tala grinned. "Oh, yeah. I counted about ten other guards stationed in different parts of the fortress and a dormitory of sorts where about twenty-five additional guards slept. Brac's fortress is exactly that. I looked quickly through the *duca* where Raj first met with him, and didn't find anything interesting. But we didn't think he would keep papers like this just lying around." Here she stopped. Mica was not going to like this next part.

"I noticed a door on the second level with two guards stationed outside so I went in. It was Brac's private sleeping chamber and he slept alone." At Mica's exclamation, Tala hurried to add, "He never woke up, Mica. I looked around his chambers and noticed a door to a small room at one end with a lock on it. I could sense a woman locked inside. She had also been beaten. I think we need to assume she is not his true mate, but the woman Ahnika talked about."

"You're probably right. So you didn't find any of the documents we might need?" Mica started to reassure his mate but she interrupted.

"I didn't say that. After I checked out the woman, I started to leave when I noticed another door on the other side of Brac's bed. This door had psychic shielding on it, which made me even more curious. The shields didn't prevent me from entering. But I went in and came out quickly, watching to make sure Brac didn't sense anything. When he stayed asleep, I went back inside wondering if this guy had another woman locked away. Only this room turned out to be another *duca*. I couldn't open any of the drawers or pick up anything but I could look at the papers on his desk. There was a paper that had Ahnika's name on it and what looked like notes from the Hunters who'd grabbed her. It mentioned they'd found her in Vidar but had lost her trail." She paused. "There was no mention of Raj on the note."

"Maybe they didn't realize it was Raj that took Nika from them?" Tar questioned and looked to Raj for an answer.

Raj shook his head. "No. They saw me. I was slightly disguised but I have met these two before. I was close enough for them to get a lock on my aura so I am sure they knew they had battled with me. But they apparently didn't share the information with Brac," he stated.

"Do you think we would find documents on the other women in this room, Tala?" Nika asked expectantly.

"Yes. I found a blank document on the table as well. There were places on the paper for a woman's name and mate information. Name, social ranking and city of origin were all blank lines to be filed in. I think everything we need to find the other women will be in this private chamber. There was another interesting list on the desk, an accounting of other women who, at one time or another, escaped. It looked like several life cycles ago seven women staged some sort of a breakout, and this list was their names and what looked like speculation on where they went. One woman's name had the words 'found and terminated' beside it," she said sadly.

The sad press of silence once again filled the room, unfortunately the only conclusion they could draw on what the words meant, depressed them all. For at least one woman, help had come too late.

"Do you remember any of the other names on the list?" Nika asked gravely.

"Hmmm, Anala…"

Nika cried out, "Jandai! I forgot I overheard one of the village women mention Brac, some of the women of the village must have escaped from him."

Raj flinched.

Nika noticed her mate's reaction. "You followed me to Jandai didn't you, Raj?" she asked carefully.

Raj closed his eyes for a *minon*, gathering his thoughts. He wasn't sure how much of this he wanted to share with the others.

"Those are the women who captured you before you were bitten by the *Nej*?" Mica asked.

"What's a *Nej*?" Nika asked.

Shivet, like he could keep any secrets from this group. Letting his breath out slowly, he decided it didn't matter, if Nika could share what she had been through, he could as well. "Okay, not that I am really happy about sharing this story but I followed Nika to this village, Jandai. It is comprised of a group of women and as far as I know, there are no men in the village. Do you know how many women lived there, Nika?" he stopped to ask.

"You are right, there are no men and I think there are over twenty women. Raj, I am so sorry they got a hold of you."

"Twenty-five, I counted them...and it's not your fault, sweet one. And in some weird, psychotic way what they did to me makes sense now if some of them had escaped from Brac. I don't need to go into details but those women are crazy. They will need a lot of help."

"Many of the women are militantly anti-male," Nika said. "One group developed a potion they thought would allow them to conceive children without mate bonds and they planned to capture men to use as... Oh, Raj!" she exclaimed in horror and turned to her link mate, her hand covering her mouth and her eyes huge.

Raj pulled her onto his lap and wrapped his arms around her, quietly soothing her. "It's okay, love. Finding you made everything worth going through," he whispered into her ear. Holding her tight for a long *minon* he then said to the rest of them, "Right after I escaped from the women is when the *Nej* bit me."

Mica filled the silence by explaining to Nika what the *Nej* was and how its bite kept Raj off her trail for over a *setnon*.

"At some point, we will have to send an emissary to Jandai and help the women if they will take assistance and do something about the potion," Tar noted.

"Yeah, but I would suggest it be all women—maybe Shalan wouldn't mind getting involved," Mica noted.

Tar and Nyssa took turns explaining her idea of forming Hunter-healer groups to find the women. "I will be contacting Shalan as soon as it's light," Nyssa said.

Mica looked out the window. "Which is coming soon. I think maybe we all need a break. Let's get some rest and think about our next steps. Nyssa can get a hold of Shalan in a few *nilts* and we can all meet back here at mid-suns and figure out how to get the women and papers away from Brac," he said, standing up with Tala cradled in his arms. "Tala is worn out and we all need to be at our peak this next moons rise. I don't think we can wait much longer to finish this."

"Wait!" Tala cried out, "I forgot something. There was an invitation on Brac's desk with his address and the date of next moons rising. It looked as if Brac had issued it and the place for the meeting was listed as his fortress. It was for a *glindash*. What is a *glindash*?"

Nika said sorrowfully, "It is what he called his auctions."

"Don't worry, Nika love, he won't be having another one." And Raj took her to their chambers.

Chapter Eleven

ॐ

Nika couldn't get Raj's story of his time in Jandai or the thought of him being bitten by the *Nej* out of her mind. He had been through so much for her. She tried to think of something she could do to show him how much she loved and appreciated him.

Smiling, she felt for the little scrap of clothing in her dress pocket. Well, there was always that!

Turning to him as they walked into their chambers, she sweetly asked, "Raj, Nyssa had a small bathing pool in her chambers filled with air bubbles Tar somehow fashioned for her. Do you think you could do the same with ours? I would like to relax in it before we rest."

"Bubbles," Raj murmured to himself. He'd been thinking of how he would ensure Nika stay out of any rescue mission. The thought of what Brac had done to Ahnika and his own experience in Jandai, along with the very real vision in his mind of how much worse things could have been for his mate, made him frantic to protect her. Contemplating her request, he absently slid his hand down his chest and watched Nika's eyes follow the motion. Bubbles sounded just right.

Nika grinned when Raj turned away and went into their bathing chamber. Quickly she took the *bikini* thing from the pocket of her dress. When Nyssa had conjured them earlier, both she and Tala had asked to keep them. She just knew Raj would find the small garment interesting. Stripping off her dress, she tied the undersized green triangles around her hips and over her breasts. What little there was of the fabric matched her eyes perfectly.

She heard Raj call out to her that the bubbles were ready and she moved into the bathing chamber. Standing with his back to her, he lit candles and messed with the water. He had taken off his vest and she stood transfixed at the sight of her mate's golden skin and rippling muscles. The Goddess had definitely blessed her with this man. Moving up behind him, she smoothed her hands over his shoulders. "I love you, Raj," she said softly.

His muscles tensed and he turned to pull her into his arms. "Ah, Nika. And I love you. I think I fell in love with you before I even met you," he sighed and cupped her cheek as she nestled into his hand. Moving his right hand to her other cheek, he brought his face to hers. Lowering his mouth to cover hers, he moved his hands down her arms, feeling naked skin and small strings. Frowning he pulled back from her sweet lips to look between their bodies and what he saw made him step back.

"By the moons, Nika, what have you got on?" His mate stood in front of him with two small green triangles barely covering her nipples. The full red-skinned globes of her breasts spilled out around the tiny fabric that seemed to be held tentatively in place with strings around her back and neck. Her glorious woman's curls were also barely covered by a wisp of fabric between her thighs with ties at both hips. "Nika?" he growled. The sight of his mate dressed like this made his blood heat and his cock prance in appreciation.

"Do you like it, Raj?" she asked shyly. "Nyssa called it a *bikini*. She said on Earth this is what women wear when they bathe…umm…swim in public."

His eyes glazed over at the thought of his mate bathing in public with only her nipples and woman's hair covered. He would kill any man who saw her this way. He could feel the thrum of his links in his cock and the combination of their pull and the sight of his mate had him panting in anticipation. Closing the small distance between them, he shed his clothing with a thought and scooped her up in his arms. "You will only bathe with me," he commanded sharply as he stepped into the swirling water.

Nika giggled and separated herself from his arms. She moved to recline in the warm, churning water and to put some distance between them so she could study Raj's body. Her Life Companion was incredible, all hard muscle with wide shoulders, slim hips, and strong thighs. His erection rose out of its nest of dark hair to dip gently in the moving water, waiting for her. Her lips parted as she studied the enticing dark circles of his nipples. When he sat down in the water, she licked her lips and tried to send the thought of her mouth playing with those flat discs through their link connection.

Raj groaned to himself, sure the bubbles would drive him crazy. They felt like little tongues lapping at his chest. He needed to concentrate on having a conversation with Nika to make sure she understood her place tomorrow. But the sight of his wife in her green *bikini* and the feel of the water teasing his body took all thought away. He started to move toward his mate when she lifted her palm to stop him.

"You know I come from Zmar, the water planet," she hesitated while he nodded. "My people have developed many abilities with water. Not just the ability to stay underneath for long periods of time, but to also manipulate its ebb and flow," she said.

Raj frowned. What was she talking about? "What do you mean 'manipulate water'?" he asked, confused.

She smiled into his eyes and whispered, "Let me show you. Let me pleasure you." Swirling her hand softly in the water she moved within an arm's length of him. She pushed the water toward his groin without touching him with her hands and watched as the liquid heat moved to form a small tornado around his straining manhood.

Raj watched in amazement as the water encircled his cock and wrapped him in a spinning, pulsing stream. He couldn't believe how stimulating the small whirlpool was, with its ability to close tight around him and then slowly ebb open. Tight…open…tight. "Ahhh…"

Nika concentrated on the water's movement, still reaching through her links and letting both the links and the water tease her mate's body. She focused a small vibration at his nipples and penis, and guided the water to lap up along his chest and simultaneously stroke his groin.

Raj panted as the water shifted and added further torment to his flesh. He could feel his links thrum with pleasure, seemingly in tune to the water licking along his skin. His nipples rose to tight buds the water sucked into its center, the clench and release at his throbbing cock shifted, moving up and over the ripe plum head and back down to the root. "Nika!" he gasped and tried to pull her into his arms.

Grinning wickedly, she shook her head. "Not yet, Raj. I want to give you pleasure, show you how much you mean to me. Remember, I can hold my breath for a very long time…" her words trailed off as she ducked under the water and moved her head over his lap.

He could feel her warm tongue tease the slit at the head of his cock, tantalize the gold links that wound through his turgid shaft. In shock, he realized she'd also started the links to vibrate within him, sending her excitement through to mingle and build with his own. His head fell back to rest against the side of the bathing pool and he moved his hand down to lightly cup the back of Nika's head. His mate was driving him insane with that sweet mouth and her amazing water skills.

Nika played with her mate's straining organ. Licking him from balls to tip, keeping the links' vibration and water suction constant, she strove to drive him out of his mind. Her body throbbed along with Raj's as he opened the links to share in his pleasure. Moving slowly, she positioned her mouth over the tip of his shaft and pressed her lips down to wrap him in her heat. Tonguing the links' entrance, she pushed down a couple inches and then returned to lick across the links, repeating the processes over and over, keeping the cadence steady until Raj thrashed beneath her. Each time she managed to take a little more until she took all she could and he bumped against the back of her throat.

"Arghhh." Raj could barely breathe. His body thrummed and pulsed with ecstasy as Nika's hot mouth worked up and down over his cock under the water. She didn't stop to take a breath and he was ready to come unglued within her sweet heat. He tried to pull her head up but she shook him off and growled around his flesh. The sound rippling around him combined with a spiking tremor she sent through their shared link and he threw up his hands to grip the sides of the pool, leveraging his hips to allow him to pump his cock through her lips.

The hot fever built within him to a volcanic pitch. He cried out as he felt his body tense and his seed burst from his body and into Nika's mouth. She continued to ride his cock through his release and then rose before him with a smile. He struggled to get his breathing and wildly beating heart under control as he pulled her onto his lap and held her close to him.

"Goddess, Nika. That was incredible." He thought of what she had done to him with the water and smiled. Glancing over her head at a corner of the pool behind Nika's back, he concentrated for a *minon*. It didn't surprise him to realize he could make her abilities work to his own advantage.

"Nika, love," he whispered softly in her ear. "Remember I told you that when we were linked we would probably be able to share some abilities with each other?"

Nika nuzzled his neck and nodded.

"Well, it appears at least some of your water abilities have been shared with me," he murmured against the soft skin of her neck.

"What are you talking about, Raj?" she asked sleepily.

"Let me show you, love." He turned Nika on his lap to lay her back against his chest. Her head rested on his shoulder while he positioned her legs, open and draped over each of his thighs. She groaned in pleasure as he skimmed his palms slowly down her body, using one hand to capture and play with her breasts through the damp fabric covering her nipples, while the other hand dipped to swirl first in her navel and then down to comb through the curls covering her mound. Here the fabric was in his way. With a couple of quick tugs at the sides, he disposed of the barrier.

The hand at her breast cupped her weight as his thumb stroked over her nipple, causing it to bud and grow against him. The feel of his fingers mingled in and around the rasp of cloth that provided no impediment to him. The fingers in the slick heat between her thighs traced along each plump nether lip and played with her budded clit.

"Oh, that feels so good," she cried as he slowly, relentlessly pleased himself with the responsiveness of her body. He wanted to build her passion slowly, get her to a point where she demanded more from him, where she begged him to fill her. So while he teased and stroked, he kept the links' vibration to a slight hum, intending this to last.

Nika relaxed against her mate, her body boneless. She felt cherished and loved as his hands gently massaged and skimmed along her pleasure points. She enjoyed the soft slide into arousal, enjoyed feeling her nipples tighten and push against his fingers and her pussy lightly clench against his petting fingers. It was so…lovely. He wasn't in any hurry to bring her to climax and she relished the sensations of his hands moving over her. For several *minons*, it was just right.

All at once it wasn't enough for her. Nika could feel her pulse speed up, feel her body tighten and yearn for more. She started to move against his hands, wanting him to tug on her nipples harder, rub her clit faster. "Please…" she sighed.

"Please?" Raj teased her by slipping one finger into her water-slick channel and then pulling out to rub over her tight little bud. Tempting her.

"Please. More. Harder. Faster," she groaned.

"Ummm. Glad to," he whispered into her ear as he bent to pull her earlobe into his mouth and suck. With his hand inserted under the top of her bikini, he pinched his fingers together over her nipple and pulled, rolling it in tune to her gasps. "Look between your legs, Nika," he demanded softly.

"What?" she questioned dazedly.

"Look down between your legs," he repeated. Raj worked to use the water as he'd just learned to do from his mate through their link. He fashioned a pulsing stream of water to resemble a cock. "I am not sure I can make this work the first time, I may have to use you for experimentation," he said, chuckling.

Tilting her head to the side, she frowned at her mate and looked down between her legs. Sitting on Raj's lap in water up to her waist with her thighs spread wide, between her legs she could see a sturdy shaft of water poised at her vagina. It was made the same way she'd fashioned the tornado to cover Raj. She gasped and moaned as he mentally manipulated the water to push against her. She could feel it vibrate as it seeped slowly into her channel and surged to fill her completely. Rolling her hips to meet the thrusts Raj timed to the pull at her nipples. "Yesss..." she moaned as he added the pounding throb of the links within her.

Raj kept his fingers rubbing over her clit and pulling at her nipples while he fucked her with the water cock. Nika had milked him with her hot mouth and it had taken him a bit to recover, but he was quickly growing against the sliding movement of her ass as he pleasured her.

"Arghhh...please, Raj... Harder. I need more." Nika felt as if her heart would explode if she didn't get more. The sensation of Raj's fingers and the water cock kept her right on the edge of an orgasm but it wasn't enough to send her screaming over the edge. The damn water just wasn't hard enough. "Please Raj, I need you..." she cried again and wept in gratitude when he raised up her hips and slid her down over his thick, fully engorged cock. "Yesss..." she hissed. "Yes. Yes. Yes!"

Her muscles tightened around him and her body reacted, immediately thrown into the first spasms of orgasm. Raj's hands held her still as she pulsed around him. Kept her motionless as he shifted underneath her and flexed...began to plunge his thick girth in and out of her. He increased the tempo and power of his penetrations and she moaned in concert with every deep plunge of his cock invading her core.

Digging up and into her, Raj threw his head back, the muscles in his neck constricting as he roared in ecstasy, and filled her with a powerful spurt of hot seed.

Her cries followed, and they collapsed together.

Raj decided he *definitely* liked the bubbles.

* * * * *

Nika rolled her eyes and stuck her tongue out at Raj's back. Unquestionably he had gotten up on the wrong side of the bed. Raj's pronouncements and demands started the *minon* they woke up and continued nonstop.

She wasn't to be involved in any of this moons risings' activity.

She wouldn't participate in the rescue.

She wouldn't be allowed to help recover the papers.

She wouldn't be allowed anywhere near the fortress or Brac or the women.

It didn't matter to him if Tar and Mica couldn't control their mates, he would not allow his mate to put herself in any danger.

Nika felt her eyes crossing. She watched Raj pace from one side of the room to the other and dictate to her what she couldn't do and how she would obey him. She remembered what Tala had said. *"You just wait until you want to do something Raj doesn't want you to do, then tell us again how he won't use the links."* Well, he hadn't used them to try and sway her thinking yet, he was just ranting. Remembering Nyssa's assurance that she could use the links to make him see her side, she decided maybe she should beat him to it. It was worth a try.

After all, she'd used them a little last night, but only to increase his pleasure. Wondering if she could keep him immobilized like Nyssa explained she had done to Tar, she didn't think she had the mental strength to control him for more than a few short *minons*. But she was going to have to try something soon. Her mate was not allowing her to make one comment and she couldn't even start to explain how she felt about participating. Now he was talking about putting her in a room with armed guards. *I don't think so*, she muttered to herself.

Nika thought about how the links felt in her body and mentally reached down through the physical chains to touch the psychic threads binding her to her mate. She could feel their two souls join together and she could also see her own pulsing red and blue aura as it mingled outside her body with Raj's gold and green. Pushing thoughts down both the links and the soul tendrils, she wound threads of her need for skin against skin and thrusting heat with remnants of Raj's carnal urgings.

Raj fell silent in mid-rant. Nika looked at him and noticed he was standing there looking at her in confusion, his body showing the beginning signs of arousal—if the growing bulge between his thighs was any indication. She kept a surreptitious thrum of longing broadcasting through the links and worked out what she would do next. Raj had said they could share powers or use each other's powers like he had learned from her to manipulate the water last night. She tried to figure out through the link she shared with him how she could...ahhh.

Raj shook his head. The mating heat was on him again and he didn't have time for the distraction. He needed to make sure Nika understood she would be staying out of harm's way in the *nilts* to come. They were supposed to be going to a planning meeting in a few *minons* and he wanted her to realize he would take no chances with her life. But the sensations pulsing over his skin felt sooo good he closed his eyes to enjoy them for just a little while and missed the sight of his mate moving around the room to pull a few things from his Hunter supplies.

He felt her hand glide over his chest and push against him, guiding him to their bed. "We don't have time," he started to protest, but a shooting spark of ecstasy hit his cock and he lost his train of thought as he fell backward onto the bed.

Nika poured sensual heat through the links and used Raj's momentary preoccupation with the sensations to tie his hands and feet to the bed with Zmarian knots — knots she had learned while sailing in Zmar with her uncle and cousins. Fishermen's knots that couldn't be broken easily, especially when the rope she used was one of his Hunter ropes. She knew the ropes had been psychically strengthened to keep anyone from escaping their bonds. A momentary flash of him being tied just this way by the women of Jandai changed her plans and she decided tying his hands would be enough. For this incident, she would leave his clothes on as well, as she didn't want him reliving that experience. She just wanted him to listen to her.

She stopped the links' torment and crawled up to straddle his hips. "Raj, listen to me," she said. He looked up at her with passion-glazed eyes and smiled wickedly.

"We are going to have to hurry, sweet. The others are waiting for us," he said as he thrust his hips against her soft heat.

He didn't appear to have any problems with being tied to the bed. Gasping, she fought to keep her thoughts on what she was trying to do. Moving forward on his stomach and off the hard ridge of his erection...helped. "Listen to me, Raj," she demanded putting her hands on either side of his face and holding his gaze with her own. "I didn't do this for your pleasure. However, I may want to tie you up later and repeat the position... I did this so you would shut up and listen to me!" she exclaimed. "I will not be kept here in the palace with an armed guard while you and everyone else go to rescue those women. I promise I will be careful, but I *will* be included. This is very important to me and I will not be left behind."

Raj frowned and worked to get his throbbing body under control. He realized now that she'd used the links to distract him so she could make him listen to her. He winced as he realized he probably hadn't heard anything she said earlier while he was listing his demands. "But, Nika, I can't take the risk of Brac getting his hands on you again. He could grab you and try and make a run for it, or if there is fighting you could be hurt," he said earnestly.

"I know, Raj, and I don't want to give him a chance to get near me again. But those women will need me. I alone know what they have gone through and some of them might recognize me and allow me to help them. If you and Tar and Mica go thundering to the rescue, the captive women will only run or try to hurt themselves...or you. They will not be expecting any man to be coming to help. They have developed an abject terror of men and I am not going to back down on this, love. Those women will be scared and I need to be there to help in any way I can."

Raj, where are you? We are all waiting for you in Tar's chambers.

Raj sighed and sent a quick message to his brother. *Give me a few* minons...*I am a little tied up right now.* With the silence came the knowledge that his very psychically powerful brother had used those powers to *see* into his room.

Mica, he growled in embarrassment.

His brother laughed in his mind and replied, *Whatever she wants just give in to her now. Somehow, the three of us ended up with women who have a fascination for tying us up to get their way. Believe me, little brother, both Tar and I have been there and there is no use fighting them. We will expect you soon.*

Mica's laughter echoed in his mind as he looked up at his mate.

"Raj, what are you doing? Are you listening to me?"

"Yes, but I was also talking to my obnoxious brother. He assures me I should just give in to your demands because I will end up doing it anyway."

"You can talk to Mica in your mind?" she asked.

"Well, yeah. I can—" *—talk to you in my mind, love. Our link bond mentally ties the two of us and Mica and I are tied by birth. I think Mica is powerful enough he can talk to anyone.*

Oh, Raj this is so cool. While we are in the fortress tonight rescuing the women and capturing Brac, Mica can help us keep tabs on each other.

Raj mumbled his displeasure. "All right. Let me up and let's go see what kind of danger I can put my mate in. This makes no sense, Nika."

She just grinned and leaned over to untie him, able to be very understanding of his mood, as she had won this argument. Her position put her breast next to Raj's mouth and he took the offered treat and pulled through the fabric of her gown and bit her nipple. "Ah...would you be willing to try these ropes later?" she sighed.

"Oh, yeah!" he answered. "As long as I get a turn to tie you up as well."

She shuddered as she thought about being tied and at Raj's mercy. "Sure, ummm, that would be great," she gasped as his hands grabbed her and he swept her underneath him for a passionate kiss. *We really need to join the others.*

"I know, I was just giving you a taste of what you can expect later," he replied as he moved off her and escorted her from the room.

Chapter Twelve

ဢ

After a heated discussion, it was decided the women *would* participate in the raid on Brac's fortress. There were three objectives in the assault this evening. They needed to release the women in the caverns and the women at the *glindash*, capture Brac and any men present to bid on the women, and recover Brac's papers which, hopefully, would lead them to other women who'd been previously sold by Brac.

Nyssa, Tala and Nika would not allow their mates to relegate the three of them to paper collection. They made the point loud and clear that they would divide up and be a part of each team. A point their mates finally and reluctantly conceded.

Mica and Tar hid in the dark outside the fortress with Nyssa. Before they left the ruling place, Nika remembered that at the one auction she'd been forced to attend, the men dressed in dark hooded robes—probably to keep their identities hidden. Mica and Tar hoped they would be able intercept three of the invited members to the *glindash*, turn the men over to waiting members of the palace guard for further questioning, and arrive at the last *minon* with invitation in hand and no time for Brac to discover they weren't who they were supposed to be.

This part of the plan held the most danger and Tar was furious with himself for not being able to prevent Nyssa's participation. Several *setnons* pregnant with their first child, he was crazy with the need to keep her out of the coming battle but she refused to listen to reason. Sighing long and

189

loudly, he knew from experience if he tried to force her away from this, she would somehow show up anyway. The best he could manage was to keep her close by his side so he could protect her.

"Someone's coming," Nyssa whispered excitedly.

"You will stay behind me and let Mica and me handle the situation," Tar turned and threatened his mate in a low voice. He was not happy with Nyssa, again he told himself that he should have been stronger, his mate should be home where she was safe from any harm.

"But…"

"No, buts…you promised to obey every…"

"Tar, here is the robe. I've already fashioned one for myself, use this as the pattern for you and Nyssa," Mica stated sarcastically. While Tar and Nyssa were arguing, Mica had surprised the man wearing the robe and turned him over to the waiting guards. Mica stood there dangling a robe from one hand and the invitation to the *glindash* in the other.

Tar wisely decided to step into the shadows with his mate and let Mica handle the next two men. With his mind, he crafted robes matching the one taken from the first man. Soon three men were on their way to the palace holding cells and they only needed to wait a few *minons* more before they presented themselves at the fortress. They wanted to be the last ones to arrive.

Raj, Nika and Tala watched with their contingents of guards as the three hooded figures made their way to the fortress doors. They held their breath as the group was escorted inside. Nothing happened. No cry of alarm, no door opening with Mica, Tar and Nyssa being thrown out to the street. Nothing.

We are in. Mica's voice whispered through all three of their minds. The strongest psychically, the raiding parties decided that Tala and Raj would mind speak to the team through Mica. He alone could simultaneously project information to the rest of the team with little effort. *They didn't look at more than the invitation and we are being escorted down a long hall to a large chamber to the right of the entrance door. They have already started.* Mica hesitated. *There are two women at the front of the room.*

Two women — that left four in the underground chambers if Tala's count was correct. Tonight, the shields around the fortress had been lowered, the low psychic barrier wouldn't prevent Raj from location-shifting Nika and their three guards along with himself, into the underground bathing chamber. Since he'd already been in the room and it was beyond the corridor Brac's guards watched, it should be safe to shift them all in at one time. Glancing over to the other team, he nodded at Tala. She too, had the ability to shift and she would take her guards into Brac's chamber. Because she'd used far-sight and *been* through those rooms in her mind, it was felt she would have no problems.

Raj made Nika stand behind him and put her hands on his waist. One guard stood behind her and reached a hand over her shoulder to place it on Raj's back and each of the other two guards stood on either side of him effectively blocking Nika from all sides, the orders were to protect her at all costs. A quick glance at Tala told him his brother had the same idea for his mate. Tala looked disgruntled but she had one guard in front of her and two flanking her back as they prepared to shift.

"Good luck, Tala," Nika called out softly.

And, then, they were in the bathing chamber.

We are in the bathing chamber and there are only the two guards down here as we had hoped, Raj projected the thought to Mica.

Tala's in, Mica relayed Tala's progress to everyone. *There is no one in the bedroom and both doors are locked. They're going to try for Brac's mate first.*

* * * * *

Tala carefully surveyed the door before her, allowing her senses to reach into the room. There was definitely someone in there, the trick would be to get into the room and subdue him or her before they raised an alarm. Hopefully, they wouldn't want or be able to contact Brac with their mind. The lock was simple, and it took one of the guards only a *minon* to breach it. Tala slowly eased the door open and looked around it. As she had suspected, there was a woman asleep on the bed. The same woman Tala had seen Brac bring to her claiming ceremony. Suspecting the woman to be Brac's mate, tied to him with the unnatural link chains and hopefully grateful for the chance to be free of him, Tala didn't want to make any assumptions.

Quietly she walked over to the bed as she motioned the guards back. She didn't want the woman waking and seeing several large men looming over her. Tala moved to place her hand firmly over the woman's mouth and shook her lightly, saying, "Don't be afraid. I am Tala, Mica's mate. I am not here to hurt you." Tala paused as the woman came to startled awareness and looked at her from wide, fearful brown eyes. The woman would be pretty if she didn't look so, well...worn. "If I take my hand away will you scream for help?" Tala questioned.

The woman shook her head no and Tala could feel Mica move in her mind. *She is telling the truth.* Mica was monitoring her. *Of course Mica is monitoring me,* she knew better than to think he'd leave her without his support no matter what else he was supposed to be doing.

Tala took her hand from the woman's mouth. "Are you Brac's true life mate or one of the women he has embedded with false links?" Tala asked bluntly.

The woman's eyes widened further and she looked frantically around the room, her body went rigid when she saw the guards at the door.

"They are with me and they will not hurt you. In case you don't recognize the outfit they are wearing, they are Tar's private guard. We are here to stop Brac and the auction he has taking place below."

"He will hurt us all when he finds you here," the woman said sadly. "You must hurry and leave. There is no hope for me, I have been bound to him for almost five life cycles."

Tala sucked in her breath and asked again, "Truly bound or false linked?"

The woman's eyes filled with tears and she sobbed, "These chains did not come freely from my body. But it won't matter. As long as he holds the device that governs them, he has the power to kill me with the touch of his hands."

Tala gasped, "The black boxes can kill through the false links?" She immediately checked to see if Mica was still monitoring this conversation and she could feel her mate waiting for the answer.

"Yes, I have seen him use the device to kill a woman who refused to obey him," she said sadly.

Ask her if each woman has their own device or if one box works on all? Mica's question moved urgently through Tala's mind.

"Does every woman Brac has embedded with the false links have to have her own box device or will one device work on all women?"

The woman frowned as if she were having trouble understanding the question, then her eyes cleared. "One device works on only one woman," she stated. "But you must get out of here before Brac or someone else finds you here," she went on urgently.

"What is your name?" Tala asked gently.

"Zabeth."

"Zabeth, do you wish to be free of Brac?"

"I don't think that is possible," she replied dejectedly. "I have tried to escape before, and this time he would simply kill me rather than beat me for any trouble I cause."

Tala laughed softly, "Oh, no...Brac will never get his hands on you again. This I can promise you. I am not alone tonight. Brac's reign of terror will end this moons rise and we will see you are rid of your false links and this man. I need to get the papers Brac has in the *duca* beside his bed. Will you dress and help me in this?"

"You would be able to take these horrid chains from my body?" Zabeth asked excitedly.

"I believe so," Tala replied. "My mate and the Selven High Priestess will work together to heal you and all the other women we recover. We have already made arrangements for this. Now, I ask again, would you rather just wait with one of the guards until it is safe to leave or will you help me?"

The woman sprang up and gleefully clapped her hands. "I would love to help you! Oh, how I would like to help bring about his fall. Let me just throw this robe on, I do not want to take anything from this house but what you need." Zabeth jumped up and threw an old robe over her naked body.

Tala caught a glimpse of bruised skin. "Are you up to this?" she asked with concern.

"If it gets me out of this place, I am up to walking many legions," Zabeth said with fervor. "Just tell me what you need me to do."

* * * * *

Mica relayed Tala's success in freeing Brac's "mate" to everyone and turned his attention back to watching the room. Nyssa had maneuvered herself close to the women, Tar wasn't far from her and Mica slid into position across from Brac. There were six additional men present to bid on the women and two guards hovered in the back of the room. Mica didn't like having only himself, Tar and Nyssa to deal with nine men.

Without the three women present, it would have been a different feeling—he would have relished the fight. But he and Tar would have to divide their attention between protecting the women and subduing the men. He had no idea what talents or weapons any of the nine might have and so he would wait as long as he could, giving the other two groups time to finish their jobs and send reinforcements.

Everyone's attention focused on the small stage at the front of the room where two women, scantily draped in sheer blue fabric, were being displayed. So far Brac allowed the women to just stand there, heads bent while the men circled around them. Brac issued a decree that they weren't to be touched...yet.

Mica would not allow them to be touched, period. He would wait as long as he could for the others. When they were able, they would send their guards to come assist at the *glindash*. His first priority was to find the small black devices that controlled the women's false links. Mica refused to allow them to suffer any more pain than they'd gone through already and the discovery of how the devices could be used to kill the women made their recovery more urgent. He would assume either Brac or one of the guards had them, and worked to find them before any battle began.

Raj moved silently out and along the corridor to position himself behind one of the guards at the entrance to the dark, cell-lined passage. Thankfully, this area was dimly lit and the men were facing the cells. The only noise he could hear was soft sobbing coming from one of the prison rooms down the long, dark corridor. The thought of Ahnika being kept in such a way for two life cycles horrified him.

Both men would have to be taken out quickly and without any chance they could somehow raise an alarm. Tar's palace guards could fight and defend using psychic powers as well as more traditional weapons but, if they fought, there would be too many opportunities for Brac's guards to alert him.

It had been decided Raj would try and use a restraining shield on the men. If they possessed little psychic power of their own, it would immobilize them and block any telepathic message they tried to send. The risk came if one or both were too strong for his shield to work. Well, all he could do was try and, if the shield failed, counter with a more physical attack.

Raj went completely still and focused his mind, working to build a protective screen of golden light. He watched as a dome coalesced in front of him and he mentally pushed it to cover both men. And waited. Neither man shifted nor spoke, but stood in rigid silence. They hadn't been moving much before so maybe this wasn't a good indication that his shield worked. Carefully Raj moved to stand in front of the two men with his flash wand drawn. He would kill them if he had to.

When both men stood completely immobilized, he smiled with the realization he wouldn't have to kill them. They didn't so much as blink when Raj placed himself before them—they were frozen and incapacitated. Testing the strength of the shield, he lifted his hand and pushed against it and was rewarded with no movement. Glancing over the men, he saw no keys or any evidence of torture devices.

Locking the shield in place, he called to Nika and the guards and watched to make sure the safeguard held firmly in place as they joined him.

Leaving two palace guards to watch over the captive men, he and Nika began their search for keys to unlock the cells. Finding the actual keys would be faster than using psychic power to unlock each room and they wouldn't run the risk of Brac sensing a disruption in the psi-alarms. If he'd bothered to set them.

"Here," Nika whispered excitedly. "I think these must be the keys." Nika turned from one of the open chambers with a ring of keys in her hand. Raj glanced in the room and clenched his jaw. It was the chamber Nika described being taken to on a number of occasions. A room with arm and leg shackles attached to the walls and an assortment of whips and other pain-causing instruments scattered about. Being confronted with the reality of her past experiences almost brought him to his knees. If he did nothing else, he would see this building destroyed as soon as possible. The psychic pain emanating from the walls would make it uninhabitable anyway.

Turning, he followed Nika down the hall and stopped her when she came to the first cell door. "Don't bother with that cell, there is no one in it."

"Which then?" she asked.

"Here." Raj pointed as he took the ring of keys from his mate and worked to find the right key. Slowly he opened the door and glanced in to ensure the occupant was female and would be no threat to his mate before he let her in before him.

"Don't be afraid," Nika called softly into the room. "We have come to rescue you."

Chapter Thirteen

80

Mica sighed. It was done. The women in the chambers below had been released from their cells and moved onto the waiting transportation *cids* along with Brac's false mate and several boxes of papers which appeared to contain information to help them find the women already sold into mate bondage. Tala and Nika had been convinced to accompany the women back to the Ruling Place. They had gone very reluctantly.

The time had come to finish this.

Before Mica could intervene, Brac moved to the women on the platform and said, "The proceedings will start. I will, of course, demonstrate the women's submissive training and how you can control them. After this example, you will be allowed to examine the attributes of each woman much more closely." At this, he leered out at the crowd and moved to pull two controlling devices from a robe pocket. "I am happy to say if you don't find anything you like this *bi-non*, I have several additional females who will have completed their training by the next full moons and I should also have a couple new females delivered to me by the end of the *setnon*."

This gave Mica pause. Brac claimed he had more women being captured and he hadn't even considered that possibility. *Shivet!* How could they find out where Brac's men were raiding and stop them from gathering more women? It would have to wait, as he couldn't contemplate the future now. At the *minon*, he needed to stop this nightmare.

Mica concentrated on the boxes in Brac's grasp and pulled with his mind. *Yes!* He had them within his own hands.

Brac yelped as the boxes flew from his hand and into Mica's. "Who dares..." he started to demand when he saw the tall robed figure and watched with a look of disbelieving anger as Mica lowered his hood and Brac realized who threatened him.

"Brac, you are under Royal Zylan arrest for the crimes you have committed here," Mica stated darkly. "As are all of you present for being involved in the torture and torment of these women."

Before Mica finished his pronouncement, Brac screamed in rage and the air in the room trembled in reaction to the power he unleashed. Violent blue arcs of lightning flew from his hands and clashed with the shields of energy Mica rapidly projected. Without taking his eyes from Brac, Mica knew Nyssa had pushed the women to the floor and was hovering over them. "Tar!"

"Got it. Focus on Brac."

Mica smiled as he felt the pulsing force of a protective shield flow over all three—Tar had seen to the protection of the females. Without dividing his concentration, he added another layer of strength to the psychic safeguards over Nyssa—nothing could be allowed to happen to her, she carried the future of Zylar in her womb.

Chaos arose within the chamber as the men either tried to flee or joined in the fight. Mica grinned as Raj appeared suddenly with several palace guards to join in the fight. Returning his attention to Brac, he saw the man's face was strained with the effort he poured into throwing the sizzling bolts of energy. Mica played with him a bit, hampered because he didn't want to kill Brac, but sought to keep him alive for questioning. So he worked on countering Brac's mental onslaught while keeping damage to a minimum.

Mica's robe shredded easily from the psychic strikes and small streaks of blood appeared across his chest. *Tala was going to be upset.* Brac seemed to crow with his assumed victory. Mica's muscles bulged with the power he harnessed as he aimed a brilliant ball of focused energy toward Brac. Shrieking in pain, Brac fell to the floor while trying to shift his form. Mica could only assume he intended to try and fight as an animal predator. With a flick of his wrist, Mica settled a dark cloud over Brac, preventing any shape shifting and knocking him out cold.

Mica quickly fashioned a restraining collar from the air around him and placed it around Brac's neck. The collar would keep Brac from using any psychic abilities and, if he tried, the collar would cause extreme pain. Mica hoped he would try. It would give the man a taste of his own depravity. Then he bound Brac's arms and legs with Zylan restraints and turned him over to one of the palace guards.

He checked to make sure the shield still kept Nyssa and the two women sheltered in its protective embrace and then turned to watch as Tar and Raj battled the remaining men. Brac's two guards had disappeared. Mica knew the sentinels Tar placed around the fortress would make sure they didn't escape justice, so he didn't worry about them.

Two other men were unconscious on the floor, Mica moved to restrain them so they couldn't wake and rejoin the fight or flee the melee unnoticed.

Raj backed another two men into a corner and played at trading psychic shocks with them. Deflecting those shocks sent toward his body, he gleefully returned the sharp energy with an added bite. He was in no danger.

Tar had one man psychically pinned to the wall while he used his fists against the other. Mica laughed out loud, his deep chuckle sounding very strange in the room. A quick glance at Nyssa told Mica that Tar's mate enjoyed the fight. She'd shifted to a sitting position within the protective bubble and mimicked her mate's actions by throwing punches at the air. Tar had indeed found his true mate.

Tar had always preferred to fight with his fists. He said he liked the satisfaction of hearing the smack of skin against skin. Mica had better help the poor man before Tar beat him to death. Moving up to Tar, he tapped him on the shoulder. As Tar turned to him, the man he was fighting threw another punch. Mica caught the hand in his own grip and quickly dropped the man into a sound sleep. Swiftly fitting the fallen man with restraints, he turned to Tar. "I think we are done here. Let's round up these prisoners and turn them over to the guards so they can be transported back to the Ruling Place. I will make sure Brac is settled nicely in his new quarters and join you and the others back at the palace. We still need to see to the women's health tonight or I would let you keep on pounding these poor men," Mica said with a grin.

Tar sighed. "You always like to ruin my fun, Mica. But you are right. I need to get my mate and these last two women to the palace." He glanced at Raj and grinned. "You going to tell Raj he has to stop playing?" he asked.

"Raj!" Mica bellowed. "Wrap them up in pretty little packages so we can get home to our mates before Nika and Tala start going through Brac's papers and decide they are going to go rescue someone else without us." Mica enjoyed playing with his brother, he watched as Raj turned white as a sheet and, with the snap of fingers, had his two prisoners bound and gagged.

Raj blanched, thinking Mica could be right. In a quick and efficient move, he put the two men to sleep and restrained them. All of the men except Brac were turned over to the guards. Mica would take Brac to a special psychic holding cell that could withstand any attempt he made to break free. The shielding collar would be left around his neck as a further precaution against his escape.

The next several *setnons* would be busy for all of them, Raj knew. He accepted that he and his mate would be involved with the women. Not in the healing of them, as neither Nika nor himself had healing skills strong enough to be of any help during this time, but in finding the women who were still in captivity.

But for now he would concentrate on Nika. Her family would be coming soon and within a few short *bi-nons*, they would have their claiming ceremony.

* * * * *

"I, Raj, take you, Ahnika, as my Life Companion. I hold you in my possession. I promise to put forward my life for you. Always you will have my protection. My faithfulness. You will become the vessel that holds my spirit, my essence, and, for always and evermore, my body. I take under my shelter all that is yours. Your life becomes mine, your pleasure within my reflection. You are bound to me with Companion Links for all eternity and always under my guardianship," Raj said seriously as he turned to his mate.

Nika continued with a smile, "I, Ahnika, recognize you, Raj, as my Life Companion. I carry your vow within me, remaining faithful and obedient to your needs and desires. My life is pledged to your care, my pleasure a reflection of your own. I am bound to you with Companion Links for eternity and will be always under your guardianship."

Glancing down at the beautiful deep green...and thankfully opaque gown, she said a mental *thank you* to Nyssa and Tala for having known she couldn't wear the traditional claiming gown. The customary mating attire was a burnished copper color made from extremely sheer material. The traditional gowns were *so* thin and *so* low-cut nothing was left to the imagination. They had a center slit running from the hem, up to inches before the waist, allowing everyone flashes of pubic hair. Just the thought of exposing herself in such a gown had made her cringe.

She much preferred the dress Nyssa had fashioned for her. It had the high waist she called "empire style" with a low neck showing just a hint of cleavage and no slits in sight. Nyssa had taken her aside the night before and handed her the dress, saying she had been able to make the point with her mate that if women weren't comfortable with the dress, it victimized them just as surely as what Brac had put them through. Tar had agreed without discussion, saying it was Nika's time and she could dress how she liked, and Nika would be forever grateful to the Ruler and his link mate.

She wondered at what point Nyssa would have her way in changing the words to the Claiming Ceremony now that she'd managed to have the public drawing banned and the ceremonial gown changed.

Nika had spoken to the Ruling Council last *bi-non* and told her story, as had many of the women they had freed from Brac.

Brac thought he would undermine Tar's reputation enough that one of the other planets would start a war, allowing him to take over the planet. The extent of his madness had been detailed in his papers. He'd been planning his own rebellion. Now he was locked in a cell. Brac was obviously crazy and seemed to be getting even worse, spending hours rocking back and forth and mumbling incoherent words. Unfortunately, they wouldn't be getting very much information from him, only what they found revealed in his writings.

Brac's rebellion died with a whimper but there was another Zylan rebellion—one led by the women of the planet. Brac's machinations had thrust Zylar into what Nyssa gleefully called the "feminist movement".

With a touch, Raj brought Nika's thoughts back to the ceremony. He gathered her into his arms and whispered tenderly in her ear, "I have claimed you before others as my own to love, cherish and protect. I love you, Ahnika." His mouth moved reverently over her cheekbone, nibbling until he could claim her lips.

Raj's kiss swamped her senses, plunging her into an immediate physical craving. It felt as if she hadn't been alone with him for more than a *setnon* instead of just a few short *binons*. Her family had come from Zmar and her mate understood her need to spend as much time as she could with them before the ceremony. Now she needed him. Groaning into his mouth, she could feel his hunger for her and hear the soft laughter of their families as he location-shifted them from the ceremony and into the privacy of their chambers.

"I am sorry, Nika. I couldn't wait any longer for you," he panted.

"Don't be sorry," she murmured as she worked to help him strip them both of their clothes. "Be appreciative."

He laughed as he threw her naked on the bed and fell on top of her. Leaning down, he kissed her closed eyes softly. Moving his mouth leisurely over her cheek to her nose and then resting lightly on her mouth, he caught her quiet sigh before he touched his tongue to her lips. Running it softly over the seam, he coaxed her into letting him savor her spicy, warm taste. Kissing her silently, tenderly...and, inside, he pushed through the links to share in her quivering need.

She could feel her body readying itself for his pleasure as moisture pooled between her thighs and her links thrummed.

Squirming beneath him, she tried to position the hard ridge of his shaft where she wanted it most.

But he refused her and continued to kiss her slowly, turning down her offer to join their bodies in a fast coupling. "I have waited so long for you, I need to taste and touch every inch of your flesh. Let me, Nika. Let me love you."

So he teased them both with hot, drugging kisses and by running his hands over her curves, as the links could never do. So soft, a whisper of touch as he cupped her supple breast. Weighing the feel of her in his palms, she watched and felt his thumb graze her nipple. Playing with the fragile chains threaded through the tips, rolling them. Plucking them. Nika sucked in a breath as Raj bent over her.

"Mine!" he growled. "I will never get enough of you, Nika," he panted against her sensitive skin before taking the stiff peak into his mouth. He circled her dusky burgundy areola with his tongue, simultaneously squeezing the other breast and playing at the hard nub with his fingers. Shifting over and paying homage to the other breast, he continued to use his mouth and tongue, his fingers and palm, to milk every ounce of response from her body.

Nika moaned, moving restlessly. She wanted to run her hands down Raj's body, sought to touch him the way he touched her. Moving her hands to stroke the silky-smooth length of his hair, it felt wonderful, soft and cool beneath her fingers.

Raj grabbed both of her hands and pulled them over her head, seeking to bind her writhing body with his thoughts. If she touched him, he would explode and he wanted to savor her, keep her completely under his spell. He would not stop or slow down until she begged for mercy. Fondling her, Raj escalated the links' caress.

Nika panted.

"Hold on, little one," Raj murmured into her flesh. "Let me love you with my mouth, my body. Relax and feel the immense need I have for my Life Companion."

Nika couldn't move her arms, but her head thrashed from side to side as she quivered under his spell. He spent what seemed like *nilts* concentrating his hands and mouth on her already overly sensitive breasts. She was ready to explode with just the attention he spent on her nipples. Then, slowly, he licked and tasted his way down to her belly button. Running his tongue along the chain at her waist she felt the link quiver deep within her body's core. Panting, she again tried to move, wanting to reach out and touch him in return.

He whispered against her sleek skin, "Relax and enjoy, my mate. Allow me."

Following the link down to her body's moist folds, Raj's mouth closed over her. Licking, stroking, and enjoying the surge of spicy heat he called from her center, as he dipped lower and thrust his tongue into her tight sheath he groaned at the subtle flavor between her thighs. He felt maddened by her taste, unable to stop using his tongue to flick her to peak and then lightly bite her nub to send her screaming into climax. Again and again he took her up and over then let her fall into a disjointed and sated state before starting over. Each rush brought power and strength to his *Vampen* nature, allowing the control he sought.

Using their bond, he became Nika as he shared the physical intimacy of their link with his mate. His tongue filled her and she pushed the feel of the lush pleasure of his mouth back to him along the binding ties. The overwhelming sensation tormented them both, teasing. Driving Nika to the brink. Allowing her to take Raj with her.

Nika screamed, her senses inundated with the onslaught of feeling between the links vibration and her mate's physical touch. In her mind, she felt his cock swell and bead with moisture, as if his body were hers. She could taste herself on his tongue and feel his need for her. He was making her crazy and finally she sobbed, begging him, "Please. Please, Raj, I can't take any more. Please?"

Raj took one last long suck on the sweet nub between her thighs and as Nika soared into yet another orgasmic spasm, he climbed up her body to lay over her. Draping her leg up over his thigh he carefully parted her with his throbbing manhood. Pushing forward into her tight sheath, he tilted her hips back to allow him to plunge deep. He stopped to slide his thumb from where they were joined together, brushing lightly over her clit. "More!" he whispered loudly and within her mind. *More!*

Nika gasped and tried to use her body to force him to movement.

"Take it slowly, little one," he groaned as he felt her inner muscles tighten around his length. She was so tight and sweet. The links vibrated and he cried out as the collective sensations swamped him. He shared her mind and her body's reaction to his invasion, the combination of her need and his own overwhelmed him and he lost control.

Finally. Nika's thought screamed through his mind as he started to move. Hard and fast he thrust into her. Slap. Slap. Slap. Their bodies came together as their minds communicated the building waves of pleasure. The force of his assault left her breathless and stunned. He filled her so deeply! Too soon, she felt his cock strain and burst as he flooded her with his release. She would never get enough of her mate.

* * * * *

Later, much later, they would talk about the future. Raj knew Nika would not be happy unless she could be involved in searching for all the missing women. But for this short time, he had an excuse to shut out the rest of the planet. He had a mate. They'd shared their ceremonial bonding this *bi-non*, the next moons rise was soon enough to look forward to the challenges of their life together.

About the Author

ಐ

Ravyn Wilde was born in Oregon and spent a carefree childhood in places like New Guinea, Australia and Singapore. She is married, has three children and lives in Utah. Ravyn is happiest when she has a book in one hand and a drink in the other—preferably sprawled on a beach somewhere!

Ravyn welcomes mail from readers. You can write to her c/o Ellora's Cave Publishing at 1056 Home Avenue Akron OH 44310-3502.

Read an excerpt from:

LET THEM EAT CAKE

Copyright © RAVYN WILDE, 2005.

Let them eat cake…

A hedonistic and sarcastic rebuttal to the unsolicited information her peasants were starving, those words had been splashed across the newspapers of the day, accompanied by a very unflattering drawing. Her enemies had used the phrase to define her and even her friends believed her capable of the sentiment. That one sentence had followed her through all the years of her life and death.

What a bitch!

She'd been a royal pain in the butt—self-indulged, self-absorbed, a class-conscious bitch of a snob. Or so they said.

The guillotine served as her wake up call. Thank God she'd discovered Luscious Lucian's secrets and managed to seduce him into her way of thinking. She'd needed those years—two hundred and twelve of them, to be exact—to grow up. She'd only been thirty-seven when she lost her head. Still somewhat immature and self-centered, although nothing like her very public depiction. She wondered if the media campaign, designed by the French aristocrats and carried out with the sole intention of turning a nation against her, had been the first of its kind. She guessed it didn't matter now. The added centuries to her life had helped her mature and evolve into the woman who could stand here and look at the city she protected…

And have the words "Let them eat cake" stand for something far different. In her heart and soul she cared for these people. Mortal and immortal alike. She wanted nothing but the best for them.

Let them eat cake.

She no longer played the role of despotic ruler. She was Sentinel.

"Hello, sweetcheeks." The male baritone voice belonging to Matt intruded on her introspection. She loved listening to him—his voice sounded rich as molasses and dripped with sin. She turned to watch the show as the cover-model boy-toy strutted with ingrained confidence across the penthouse garden. His body all tanned perfection and muscled temptation showcased in tight black jeans and a black tank top. The hair falling around his shoulders looked golden, long and bad-boy tousled

"You are *soooo* not subservient enough," she mumbled.

"Darling, I can do subservient with the best of them. You just don't have the proper dangly bits to make it worth my while." Matt smirked as he did a little girly flip of his hair.

She hit him.

He laughed.

"Wake up on the wrong side of the coffin this evening, luv?" he questioned impudently.

She shook her head She would not explain to Matt the nightmare she'd been plagued with yesterday, or how she'd begun this night with a feeling something new—something Bad with a capitol B—had come into their area. He would only worry and nag her to death. Not to mention she would somehow have to explain to him *why* she had been dreaming. In all her centuries of undead life, she'd never dreamed. How weird was that? She was fucking two-hundred-and-twelve years old for Christ's sake, and it seemed a little ridiculous to have started that very human trait now.

She'd created a fiend the night she turned Matt into a half-ling and made him a vampyr's human servant. Two fiends, she amended, as she could hear Laurel coming to find Hardy. Brian coming to find Matt—they made the cutest couple.

She sighed. The perfect human servants for her—a weird cross between a Jewish mother and Dracula's Igor. Snorting to herself, she turned to watch the dark side of the beefcake duo as he came into sight. Her gift of nearly eternal life only enhanced what God doled out in spades at their birth. Brian was as dark as Matt was golden. He had long, jet-black hair, with moonlight pale skin and a sadistic sense of humor. The hard body was as toned and sculpted as Matt's. Her bookends.

Matt and Brian started out many years ago as fuck buddies and ended up as lifelong partners. Longer than lifelong partners, considering the fact they'd been with her for almost thirty years and didn't look a day over twenty-six—the age they'd been when she met them. In mortal years they were in their early fifties. They would age over an almost endless period of time. At least as long as she lived, they would.

"You're salivating sweetcheeks," Matt said, in a matter-of-fact tone.

"Sure I am, I'm hungry," she countered.

"Well, I am not going to be your snack tonight," Brian stated. "Go fang bang some appreciative human male."

"Wonderful idea," she said, hopping up onto the four-foot brick wall surrounding the penthouse garden space. She turned to smirk at the two of them as she leaned back into the wind and plummeted backwards off the edge. She smiled as she heard Matt's indrawn breath and his verbal cry...

"I fucking hate it when you do that!" he shouted.

Why an electronic book?

We live in the Information Age—an exciting time in the history of human civilization in which technology rules supreme and continues to progress in leaps and bounds every minute of every hour of every day. For a multitude of reasons, more and more avid literary fans are opting to purchase e-books instead of paperbacks. The question to those not yet initiated to the world of electronic reading is simply: *why?*

1. *Price.* An electronic title at Ellora's Cave Publishing and Cerridwen Press runs anywhere from 40-75% less than the cover price of the <u>exact same title</u> in paperback format. Why? Cold mathematics. It is less expensive to publish an e-book than it is to publish a paperback, so the savings are passed along to the consumer.

2. *Space.* Running out of room to house your paperback books? That is one worry you will never have with electronic novels. For a low one-time cost, you can purchase a handheld computer designed specifically for e-reading purposes. Many e-readers are larger than the average handheld, giving you plenty of screen room. Better yet, hundreds of titles can be stored within your new library—a single microchip. (Please note that Ellora's Cave and Cerridwen Press does not endorse any specific brands. You can check our website at www.ellorascave.com or

www.cerridwenpress.com   for   customer
recommendations   we   make   available   to   new
consumers.)

3. *Mobility.* Because your new library now consists of
   only a microchip, your entire cache of books can be
   taken with you wherever you go.

4. *Personal preferences are accounted for.* Are the words you
   are   currently   reading   too   small?   Too   large?
   Too...**ANNOYING**?   Paperback   books   cannot   be
   modified according to personal preferences, but e-
   books can.

5. *Instant gratification.* Is it the middle of the night and all
   the bookstores are closed? Are you tired of waiting
   days—sometimes   weeks—for   online   and   offline
   bookstores to ship the novels you bought? Ellora's
   Cave Publishing sells instantaneous downloads 24
   hours a day, 7 days a week, 365 days a year. Our e-
   book delivery system is 100% automated, meaning
   your order is filled as soon as you pay for it.

   Those are a few of the top reasons why electronic
novels are displacing paperbacks for many an avid reader.
As always, Ellora's Cave and Cerridwen Press welcomes
your questions and comments. We invite you to email us
at service@ellorascave.com, service@cerridwenpress.com
or write to us directly at: 1056 Home Ave. Akron OH
44310-3502.

THE
☥ ELLORA'S CAVE ☥
LIBRARY

Stay up to date with Ellora's Cave Titles in
Print with our Quarterly Catalog.

TO RECIEVE A CATALOG,
SEND AN EMAIL WITH YOUR NAME
AND MAILING ADDRESS TO:

CATALOG@ELLORASCAVE.COM
OR SEND A LETTER OR POSTCARD
WITH YOUR MAILING ADDRESS TO:

CATALOG REQUEST
C/O ELLORA'S CAVE PUBLISHING, INC.
1056 HOME AVENUE
AKRON, OHIO 44310-3502

And check out Ravyn Wilde's *Keeper of Tomorrows* along with five other exciting stories in the latest release

ELLORA'S CAVEMEN: LEGENDARY TAILS IV

Orgasm Fairy By Ashleigh Raine

For Orgasm Fairy Cammie Witherspoon, frustration is a way of life. She helps people deal with their sexual frustration every day, but nothing and no one can help ease her own. You see, Orgasm Fairies can't orgasm. It's part of their curse.

Crystal-eyed, dark haired, and all-over hottie Neal Fallon is determined to seduce Cammie. And even though nothing can "come" of it, she knows Neal will make her feel more than she's felt in a very long time.

Boy oh boy, is she in for a wicked good surprise.

Overcome By Marly Chance

"Have you ever been ravished?" The question uttered in that sexy masculine voice sent Ansley reeling. Held captive on a hostile planet and scheduled for interrogation, agent Ansley Morgan is shocked when her former partner appears. She is even more surprised to discover that he is supposed to be her Enraptor, paid by the enemy to forcibly seduce her into revealing information. Is he there to help her or betray her?

Secrets We Keep By Mandy M. Roth

Trisha hasn't been able to keep a lasting relationship to save her life. When one of the string of losers she dates asks her to marry him, she says yes, thinking it beats being alone. Besides, the man of her dreams doesn't view her as anything more than friend.

Dane can't get his best friend Trisha out of his head. She consumes his every thought. He's wanted her for seven years but mating with a human is forbidden. It's not every day a human learns of their existence and it's not every day a lycan gives himself over to someone unconditionally.

A Love Eternal *By N.J. Walters*

Sitting alone on a bridge late one night, Genevieve Alexander laments her safe, boring life. But when she attracts the attention of a dangerous, mysterious stranger known only as Seth, her entire world changes.

Accompanying him on his nocturnal journey through the dark streets and into the throbbing nightlife of the city, he introduces her to a world of sensual desires unlike anything she's ever experienced. But Seth has a terrifying secret. Will she be able to throw off the shackles of her past and accept the risks that come with being with this sexy, compelling man?

Keeper of Tomorrows *By Ravyn Wilde*

Raine opened her door late one night to a tall, dark haired man. A man from another dimension who swears he's waited centuries just for her. Will a passionate night of show and tell convince Raine of her destiny?

Talon needs his Keeper to accept him as the man he truly is. Their worlds, all worlds, need a matched Guardian pair to save mankind from untold evil. This may be his last chance to persuade her of what a life together might be like. He can offer her adventure, love, and his body for eternity. Will it be enough?

Seeds of Yesterday *By Jaid Black*

The wealthy and influential Hunter family never thought much of Trina Pittman. Born on the wrong side of the tracks, Trina wasn't considered a worthy choice of a friend for their daughter, Amy. Being disliked by Amy's parents had been tough on Trina while growing up, but putting up with Amy's older brother, Daniel, had been brutal. Those dark, brooding eyes of his had followed her around high school - judging her, reminding her she'd never be good enough for them. It was almost a relief when Amy was shipped off to boarding school, permanently forcing the two girls apart. Fifteen years later, Amy's tragic death reunites Trina with her past...and with Daniel.

erridwen, the Celtic Goddess of wisdom, was the muse who brought inspiration to storytellers and those in the creative arts. Cerridwen Press encompasses the best and most innovative stories in all genres of today's fiction. Visit our site and discover the newest titles by talented authors who still get inspired - much like the ancient storytellers did, once upon a time.

Cerridwen Press

www.cerridwenpress.com